DATES, DINNERS, AND OTHER DISASTERS

A CARY REDMOND SHORT STORY ANTHOLOGY

KAT SIMONS

Is one normal night out really too much to ask…?

All Cary Redmond wants is to go on a date with her new leopard shifter boyfriend. Just one normal, ordinary date. Other people go on dates all the time. Cary and Deacon should be able to manage at least one. That shouldn't be too much to ask, right?

Wrong.

Being a magical Protector complicates everything in Cary's life, including her ability to have a life. Dating and getting to know her boyfriend's family of powerful shifters is stressful enough. The last thing she needs is constant disruptions and disaster. Unfortunately, Cary's life is always full of trouble.

And when innocent people are in danger, Cary has to help.

DATES, DINNERS, AND OTHER DISASTERS

~

Kat Simons

~

CONTENTS

Introduction   xi

CARY AND DEACON (TRY TO) GO ON A DATE   1
DATE NIGHT TAKE TWO   37
THIRD DATE'S THE CHARM   75
DINNER WITH THE JONESES   99

Thank You   155
Books By Kat Simons   157
About the Author   159

To everyone just trying to have a life...

INTRODUCTION

The title of this anthology says it all. And is a pretty good reflection on the life of my magical Protector, Cary Redmond. She would just like to *have* a life around her job, but somehow work always interferes.

It's a problem I'm sure a lot of us can relate to. Although, maybe not in exactly this way.

All of these stories can stand on their own as individual reads. But they do take place during the timeline of the main novel series, which starts with The Trouble with Black Cats and Demons. There may be some spoilers involved in the first three. The fourth absolutely contains spoilers for the series. You have been warned.

This collection starts with Cary attempting to go on a date with her new leopard shifter mate, Deacon Jones. And trying again. And trying again. To say they have trouble having a successful date might be an understatement. These three stories take place between book 2, The Trouble with Ghouls and Serial Killers, and book 3, The Trouble with Leopard Queens and Shifter Wars, in the main novel series. They can each be read as standalone stories, but the true magnificence of Cary and Deacon's utter failure to do something as simple as go on a date really comes through when you read the stories in order.

The last story in the collection, the novella Dinner with the Joneses, takes place after the events of book 3 in the series, The Trouble with Leopard Queens and Shifter Wars. This is the one story in this collection that absolutely has spoilers for the main series, including direct references to some of the incidents that happened at the end of book 3. If you haven't read the main series yet, or haven't read book 3 yet, and you don't like spoilers, this is one to wait for until after you've read book 3. It is a story you can read and enjoy on its own, though, so if you don't mind spoilers or have read book 3, feel free to enjoy this one now.

In Dinner with the Joneses, we get to meet more of Deacon's rather large family, including his youngest brother Dylan, who gets his own standalone story in Romancing the Leopard (which is a crossover with my Tiger Shifters series). That paranormal romance comes out in May 2021.

All of the stories in this collection give little glimpses into Cary's life, and her efforts to get to know her new mate and his family a little better. They also reveal just how difficult that effort can be when her new boyfriend is a leopard shifter and her job involves jumping between bad guys and good guys to keep the good guys safe. But no one said being a walking, talking Kevlar vest was easy.

I hope you enjoy the collection! Thanks for reading.

Kat Simons
    April 2021

CARY AND DEACON (TRY TO) GO ON A DATE

Going on an ordinary date should not be this tough...

Despite knowing each other for two months, and surviving more than one dangerous adventure together, Cary Redmond and her leopard shifter mate have never managed a regular date. A first date.

An event which carries a significance that unnerves Cary. How can she be this worried about going to a movie with a man she's fought demons with? And seen naked.

But of course, for Portland's resident Protector, even the simple things in life prove complicated. And when someone needs her help, Cary doesn't dare avoid her job...even on a date.

ary stared at herself in the full length mirror hanging on the back of her bedroom closet, flatting her palm down her stomach in a vain attempt to quiet her jumping nerves. Why the hell was she so nervous? It was just a date. She'd been on those before. Okay, not a lot, but still. She had been out a few times with men. In public. On actual dates.

Why was she so nervous about going on a date with a man who'd claimed to be her mate two months ago? A man she'd already slept with and spent a considerable amount of time with.

Fine, so most of that time had involved chaos and mayhem and a few demons. And the possible end of the world. That was just life, right? Her life anyway. And he'd gone along with all that chaos and mayhem and helped her fight the demons. So, really, this should just be a nice dinner and movie and no big deal.

Except this was their first *official* date. Out of her house and in public in front of other people and like…a date.

"You need to stop rubbing that material," Marianne, one of her best friends and a trusted adviser on fashion, said from where she sat on Cary's bed. "You're going to add wrinkles, not rub them out."

"Sorry," Cary said, rubbing her hand over her thigh instead of her stomach.

Marianne snorted. "Girl, you have been spending time with this man for months now. Why the sudden spike in nerves?"

"I don't know." Was she whining? That had sounded suspiciously like a whine. What the hell was happening to her? "It's just a date, right? And it's Deacon. I mean, I've seen him naked."

"Lucky," Marianne said.

Cary rolled her eyes. Then laughed. Marianne was practically married, her relationship with Gina just passing the ten year mark a few months back. But *everyone* who met Deacon had that kind of reaction to him.

He was stunning. Dark hair. Golden eyes. A body to rival Greek gods and make them weep with jealous. A smile that could melt the ice caps and drown the planet. Really, he shouldn't be allowed out in public. The fact that he was a leopard shifter with a significant amount of animal magnetism only complimented his already wildly gorgeous appearance. And to add insult to injury, he was nice. He was a good man. And he had her back in a fight.

When he wasn't growling at her faery mentor, Jaxer, Deacon was just…wonderful.

It really wasn't fair. How as a woman supposed to deal with all that?

"It's just a date," she said aloud to herself in the mirror. "What could go wrong? We'll watch a movie—great first date move so we don't have to awkwardly make small talk while I'm still super nervous —and then we'll go eat. We've done that before. I can eat around him. In fact, he seems to like feeding me."

"Oh man, I'm gonna need a cold compress," Marianne said, fanning herself. "Do not say things like that out loud in my presence. I do not need any more happy thoughts about your mate."

Cary chuckled and turned from the mirror. "You're sure I look okay?"

"Since you won't let me dress you in one of my creations—"

"You threatened to put me in a leather miniskirt," Cary interrupted to remind her.

"I think this outfit is lovely," Marianne finished, ignoring Cary's interruption. "Makeup is subtle and beautiful."

"Thank you!" Cary rarely wore makeup because mostly she forgot about it, so putting any on was always a risky venture in out-of-practice testing.

"Your hair looks really nice down. You should do that more."

"I can't. It gets in the way." Her hair was longish, past her shoulders, and with the potential to be straight if she used a blow dryer. Since she spent most of her time diving around getting between bad guys and good guys, she mainly kept it pulled back in a ponytail. Simple and out of her face when she did her Protector thing.

Her job, being a magical Protector, basically meant she was a walking, talking Kevlar vest, putting herself between those who wanted to do harm and the objects of their efforts. She kept the good guys safe by standing in front of them while the bad guys try to get at them. She couldn't actually *do* much. She didn't control the magic. That came from her bosses. But she could channel the shit out of it and stand between the bad guys and the good guys until the end times. She even got paid for it.

But it wasn't the kind of job that lent itself to makeup and pretty hair styles and dressup clothes. The flowered black skirt and black silk shirt she was wearing were some of her few fancy clothes. And she typically only wore them on girls' nights when she was having fun with her best friends.

"You're sure I don't look like I'm trying too hard?" she asked Marianne again, running her hand over her skirt. It flared out from her hips, snugging in tight at her waist which was a good lock for her in general, showing off curves while balance her hips with the rest of her body.

Still… Maybe it was a bit much?

"Enough," Marianne said. "You look great. You're supposed to dress up on a date night. Stop trying to make excuses to put your jeans back on."

"I wasn't going to put on jeans. Maybe the one pair of slacks I own."

"No. You'll wear a skirt. That one. No more debate."

Marianne lowered her chin and gave Cary a look Cary wasn't prepared to argue with. Marianne was a seamstress, a magical weaver, and had the most exquisite fashion sense of all her friends. She trusted Marianne's opinion.

She didn't necessarily trust her friend's sense of humor—which was why the offer of a leather miniskirt had been rejected—but she trusted Marianne to tell her the truth.

"You're going to be fine," Marianne said. "He's crazy about you. He wouldn't have stuck around through all the demon madness if he wasn't."

Cary shrugged. "I have been dealing with a lot of demons lately, haven't I?"

"Yeah you have. But he's still here and wants to take you on an actual date. And your dogs love him."

She had to admit that was definitely a point in Deacon's favor. Especially since one of her dogs was a demon dog, one was a foo lion in retirement, and one was… Well, Fred was just a mundane mutt, but he was an enthusiastic terrier-collie cross who would have let her know if he didn't like the new guy in her life.

"Deacon is a good man," Marianne said. "Now stop messing with those non-existent wrinkles."

Cary opened her mouth and the front doorbell rang. Her eyes widened as the jumping nerves started churning in her belly again. "Shit. That's him."

"Stop worrying," Marianne said. She slid off the bed. "I'll go let him in. Mostly, so I can ogle him."

"Stop." Cary laughed again, taking a deep breath and letting it out slowly.

"It's like going to a museum," Marianne said as she left, her voice echoing back down the hallway. "You just have to admire the beauty."

Cary shook her head. Took one last look in the mirror. Let out another very long breath. And straightened her shoulders. She could do this. It was just a date.

Not like she was saving the world or anything tonight, right?

She met her own gaze in the mirror as she heard Marianne greet Deacon. The sound of his deep voice sent a shiver of anticipation through her, making her limbs feel even more weak and wobbly.

Oh boy.

2

Because Deacon already knew her pretty well, given they'd only known each other for a few months, he took her to see a superhero movie. She tried not to fidget as they waited in line at the concessions stand. But apparently she was doing a piss poor job of it.

"You okay?" he asked, leaning in close.

His scent was an assault on rational thought. The man smelled so good she wanted to just press her face into his neck and live there. His scent even rivaled the delicious movie popcorn smells.

Sometimes she wondered if that was the mate thing. According to him—she was a human so all this was new to her—he could tell she was his mate by her scent. There were pheromones and chemicals involved and some real actual consequences for him to having found his mate, like the fact that he had trouble controlling his leopard when they weren't together. For her, mostly, she just couldn't seem to get enough of him.

That fact was still pretty disconcerting.

"I'm fine," she said.

"Nothing job related, right?" he asked.

"Nope."

The Nags, her bosses, hadn't shown up to give her a last minute assignment—which was good since she couldn't have refused because she was at the beginning of a test year, a Protector thing no one had seen fit to tell her about, so she had to be on her best behavior. And she wasn't feeling any of the tingling she got along her spine when her particular brand of help was needed.

"Good," Deacon said. "I'd love a whole evening with you without interruption."

"You're with me all the time."

They'd been together for most of the day before this. He'd only left her alone to get ready for the date because Marianne had come over and insisted. Which meant they didn't even have the usual small talk: how was your day? How was work? Anything interesting happen this week?

Because of the mate thing, he hadn't really gone back to work yet. He was too dangerous to have around the animals. His family business was rescuing, rehabilitating, and rehousing animals, mostly exotics— as if he wasn't sexy and perfect enough already! As an animal lover, learning what his job was had just about done Cary in. Thanks to his current state, though, his sister had kicked him out, making him stay away from the business until his control returned.

He spent as much time with Cary as possible, which was how he kept ending up in the middle of most of her work troubles, and now that they were sleeping together, they were also spending most nights together. She'd managed some privacy because she'd insisted on it, including some girls' nights out because friends were a priority no matter what. But a part of her didn't want to be away from him—that part terrified her!—and she was happy to keep him around. Though, it did bother her that he hadn't been able to go back to work yet.

"You're fidgeting," he said, pulling her from her thoughts.

His breath brushed her ear and she shivered. Why were they here instead of at home? In bed. "Sorry. Little nervous."

He chuckled. That didn't help.

"Why?" he asked.

"Dates. I haven't done much of this lately. And it feels weird. Especially since we've been a couple for a month now."

"We've known each other longer."

"Two whole months."

"You don't count that first month as us being a couple?"

She winced. He'd known immediately they were mates. She had been a lot less certain. "We were only getting to know each other. I don't think it should count."

He slipped an arm around her waist, his big palm settling high on her hip, and all her feminine parts tingled at the contact. Geezus, he was like a drug. She shifted her jacket from one arm to the other so she could lean into him.

"Fair enough," he murmured. "So long as you consider us a couple now."

Given what they'd been doing in her kitchen first thing this morning, it was hard not to think of them as a couple.

"What do you want?" he asked, nodding to the concession counter.

Taking pity on her, she was sure. "Popcorn, of course."

"Of course."

God, his voice. She shivered again. "Stop that," she said.

"What?"

"Talking like that. Like we're in bed. We are not right now. This is a public place."

"We're about to be in a dark room. If we sit at the back of the theater, we can pretend it's not a public place."

"Stop." She groaned. How the hell were they going to get through an entire movie without getting distracted?

They moved up to the counter, which was another mercy, and he ordered their popcorn and drinks. The guy behind the counter looked like he'd been hit with a plank when faced with Deacon. Cary couldn't tell if he was scared or turned on by her mate, but whatever the reason, the poor man stuttered his way through trying to get their order.

She felt a great deal of sympathy for the concessions guy.

She had very mixed feelings when Deacon led her to the back seats of the theater, picking the darkest corner farthest from any of the other people in the room.

"I am not fooling around during the movie," she said, her voice so low only he had a chance of hearing her with his super shifter hearing.

He just smiled and leaned the bucket of popcorn toward her. Her stomach muscles tightened with lust and annoyance in equal measures. She shoved some popcorn in her mouth as the lights went down and the screen shifted from ads to previews. Deacon's quiet chuckle danced along her nerve endings like lightning.

She tried, she really tried, to pay attention to what was happening on the screen. She was pretty sure she'd want to see some of these movies in the future if she could get time around her job. But her entire body was hyper aware of the man sitting next to her. His heat, his delicious scent, the way his arm kept brushing against hers…

A ridiculous preview for a comedy of some kind was on when Deacon touched her cheek, gently turning her face toward him. She could have resisted if she'd been able to think straight. His golden eyes glowed faintly in the darkness. When he leaned in, putting his mouth close enough to hers she could feel his breath on her cheek, she completely forgot about the people surrounding them, the movie that was just starting, and pretty much anything else except feeling his mouth on hers.

How could she still be this overwhelmed by him? Would things always be this way? Would she ever be able to just watch a movie with him and not want to rip his clothes off?

She was a little worried she wouldn't be. The very idea of that, for a lifetime, was scary as all hell.

She still leaned into him, capturing his lips before he could kiss her, throwing herself into a future she'd never expected or wanted but could no longer resist. His hand came up to tangle in her hair. She settled her palm against his chest, feeling his heart pound through his shirt—he'd dressed up a little too, in dark slacks and a button down shirt, and it was all she could do not to start popping open those buttons to get at the hot skin beneath.

She was so wrapped up in the feel of his lips against hers, the sensations of his hands on her, she almost missed the tell-tale tingles running down her spine. For a moment, she just thought it was a reaction to Deacon. Then the significance hit her like cold water. She jerked back, her eyes widening.

Deacon frowned at her. "What?" he mouthed.

"Shit," she said and stumbled up, pushing past him to get to the exit, cursing as she tripped on the stupid high heels she was wearing. The warning tingles intensified and Cary's heartbeat pounded.

Someone was in trouble.

She barreled into the concessions area, trying not to fall down thanks to heels she only wore occasionally, and scanned her surroundings. It was relatively quiet, a lull when most of the movies had already started, no new ones due to start, and nothing had let out yet.

The lighting was too bright after the dark theater, the neon flashing lights from some of the video games against the wall making her blink. Fresh popcorn was popping, filling the area with a delicious smell that contradicted the fear coursing through her blood. She couldn't see the danger. But someone needed her. Now.

Shit.

As she scanned the concessions stand, the realization slowly settled in that it was completely empty. Where was the guy behind the counter? Where was the woman who'd been checking tickets near the front door? There were people outside, passing on the sidewalk, easily visible through the large darkened wall of windows at the front of the theater. And the woman in the ticket booth outside seemed to be there still.

But not a soul in the main concessions area.

"What's wrong?"

Deacon's voice made her jump. Of course he'd followed her.

"Not sure," she said, still searching. "Except someone needs my help."

He nodded to a door behind the concessions stand. It was closed and she'd assumed it was a storage room.

"I can just hear street traffic through that door," he said. "There must be another entrance into the theater through that room."

"Back loading door," she said. "Shifter hearing is handy."

The door pushed open easily, even though there was one of those lock panels that required a number code just to the right. Cold night air breezed through a room stacked with organized boxes of concession supplies. To the right was a small break area with a table and chairs, a tiny refrigerator, and a counter with a surprisingly nice single cup coffee maker. She followed the cold air to a back door.

The sounds of cursing and a muffled scream had her moving fast, rushing into the loading space behind the theater.

She wasn't always very bright about that kind of thing. She probably should have hung back and figured out what was happening before charging into the middle of things. But charging into the middle of things was kind of her entire job description and, well, after more than six years, it was a habit now.

Plus, she was really good at it.

She scooted between the concessions guy and another man before even noticing the other man. Once she was safely protecting the concessions guy, and Deacon had moved one step behind her and to the left so she could keep him safe too even as he guarded her back, she took a moment to actually assess the situation.

It took several more moments for that situation to sink in.

"What. The. Hell?" She stared at the thing in front of her, not quite believing her eyes.

The—man?—man was huge, towering over her and Deacon. His clothing, what she thought might have been jeans and a t-shirt, was torn and ragged, hanging off his body and exposing alternating patches of human skin and mottled fur. The black and gray fur raced over his body, emerging and disappearing like the fur couldn't decide if it should stay or not. His feet had burst through his running shoes and looked like giant paws with large nails tapping the sidewalk.

His face was contorted into an almost wolf form on the bottom with a long snout and whiskers, distorted jaw, and sharp teeth inside the elongated mouth. But his eyes were still very human, an ordinary shade of brown without the usual shifter glow. And the top part of his head was covered in dark brown human hair that didn't match the swaths of mottled fur running over the lower half of his face. His ears were ordinary human ears, mostly, but they moved and angled around in a way that was not typical in humans.

He opened his mouth, saliva dripping, and growled.

A second passed before she realized the growl was an actual word.

"Hungry."

Oh oh. "Uh," she said, still blinking at something she'd never seen before. "What…?" She shook her head and looked at Deacon. "Huh?"

"Werewolf," Deacon said. "From the smell. But…"

"Yeah, but… Did he get stuck halfway?"

"I think he did," Deacon murmured and shivered hard.

She couldn't blame him.

Getting stuck mid-shift wasn't something that could happen to all shifters. It depended on the species. And she'd never personally seen it happen before. Seeing someone now in this horrible situation was gut churningly awful. She could only image what Deacon must be feeling, given he was a shifter too, even if leopards weren't one of the species that could get stuck mid-shift.

The trouble only seemed to happen with the species who could turn humans into shifters, like werewolves and bear shifters. The species who were born to it—like leopards, tigers, and honey badgers—shifted as part of their biology. It was natural and not something that caused them pain or could potentially be stopped mid-process. A human who got turned into a shifter, whether by choice or accident, always had a learning curve and risk involved with making the change between forms.

Cary raised her hands, palms out toward the man. "If you could manage to stay calm, we can help you."

The man reared back, lifting a hand that had human fingers and very sharp wolf claws bursting from the tips of his fingers, and swiped at her. His hand bounced off her magical Protector shield, sending him reeling back a step. He charged forward and slammed against her shield, the impact throwing him backward so far he hit the chainlink fence surrounding the loading area.

"So much for staying calm," she murmured.

"He was gonna eat me," the concessions guy behind her said, his voice higher than it had been earlier that night.

"Don't worry," Cary said, reaching back to pat his arm without taking her eyes off the threat. "I've got you now. You're safe."

The wolfman climbed back to his feet and growled at her.

"Who are you?" the concessions guy asked. "What are you?"

"Just a concerned citizen, here to help. You'll be fine."

The wolfman charged them again, his claws extended, his mouth wide open. He slammed against her magic so hard his face turned to the side and flattened slightly, like he'd hit a window. She didn't feel the impact, but she winced at what it had done to him.

"Are you...are you a witch or something?" the concessions guy asked.

"Something," she conceded. "What's your name?"

"Bill," the concessions guy said, his voice choked. "Bill."

"Okay, Bill, here's the deal. You're going to stay behind me while I keep you safe, and my...boyfriend and I are going to figure out a way to contain the wolfman until we can get him some help. I'm pretty sure he doesn't know what he's doing. Or at least not completely."

"Know!" The wolfman roared. "Feed."

"Ew," Cary said. "We are not food. That's what the popcorn and candy inside is for."

"We have nachos and hotdogs too," Bill said quietly.

"Right. Hot dogs and nachos and popcorn and candy. Some of my favorite foods, actually."

"The nachos aren't very good," Bill said.

"The chips are nice," Cary allowed. "Cheese sauce is always tricky."

"Feed!" the wolfman said, again. And lunged for them.

Cary sighed as he bounced backward into the chainlink fence again. This was the tricky part. She could stand here forever and keep the kid behind her safe, but eventually the wolfman was going to leave to find other food.

Normally, her job was to stand here until the bad guys got tired and went away, saying some clichéd bad guy stuff like, "This isn't over, bitch!" They always called her a bitch. That was going to get offensive one of these days.

In this case, though, she really didn't *want* this bad guy going away only to find another poor hapless victim. That would be bad.

"We have a little problem here," Cary said to Deacon.

"That we can't let this guy get away because he's too dangerous?"

"Right on the money." She loved that she didn't have to explain these things to him.

The wolfman bounced off her shield again in a spray of saliva and growling. She wrinkled her nose. Gross.

"And I'm not sure what to do with him even if we do figure out a way to contain him." She paused as the wolfman charged again.

"Why isn't he able to get to us?" Bill asked, sounding more fascinated than scared now.

Cary waved that away. "Just an old trick. No big deal."

"He's not eating me, so yeah, kind of a big deal," Bill said.

"The important thing at the moment," Cary said, "is how are we going to keep him from eating anyone else? And what will we do with him after that? I mean, we can't just turn him over to the police like this. You know any werewolves that can help?" she asked Deacon.

"You guys know werewolves?" Bill asked, now sounding entirely too interested. "That is so cool."

"No," Deacon said, his voice deep. "It's not."

Cary felt Bill shiver a little and move closer to her. She couldn't blame him. Deacon could be scary when he wanted to be.

"Stop scaring poor Bill here. He's having a tough enough night."

Wolfman roared, the sound loud enough to make Cary wince.

"You shouldn't do that," Cary told him. "You'll attract the wrong kind of attention and they'll kill you. Just calm down. We're going to get you some help." Over her shoulder to Deacon, "Do we know anyone who can help?"

"My mother has more contacts in the werewolf world than I do," he said.

She tried not to react to that. Turned out his mother was a lot more important in the shifter world than he'd let on to her before. So was he. That was still a bit of a *thing*.

"But I know a pack in Colorado that take in strays," Deacon finished.

"Strays?" Bill asked.

"Humans turned into werewolves then abandoned by a pack," Cary explained. "Lone wolves are really dangerous. And newly turned werewolves, even worse." She gestured at the wolfman as he pulled himself off the concrete to charge again.

Blood dripped from a cut on his cheek. She sighed. She wished he'd calm down. He was really going to hurt himself soon.

"They don't always get the shift right," she said to Bill. "And even when they do, being outside pack structure is bad for them mentally."

"You know a lot about werewolves," Bill said.

"I just read a lot."

"Are you a werewolf?"

"Definitely not." She sighed again. She wasn't going to be able to come back to this particular movie theater. At least not for a while. Once Bill didn't work here anymore, maybe. "Got the number for that pack in Colorado?" she asked Deacon.

"I can get it. Problem is the time it'll take for anyone to get here. What do we do with him in the meantime?"

"Do the tranquilizers you use at work do anything to shifters?" His business had to rescue some huge animals sometimes. It often required knocking the beasts out to move them to safer environments.

"Something designed for a tiger or elephant might, and I repeat *might*, work on this guy. But I'm not bringing one of our vets into this situation. They're all human. At least, the ones here in Portland."

Well damn. "Can you or your sister use the tranquilizers?"

"Caitlin might be able to get the shot in if I hold the guy down."

She glanced back. Deacon's eyes were narrowed—and faintly glowing as his leopard came to the surface—as he watched the wolfman attack again.

"Can you hold this guy down?" she asked.

He gave her a look.

She rolled her eyes. "I'm not questioning your strength, big guy. I just mean he is a bit out of his mind."

"I can handle him," Deacon said, his voice very deep now.

Her turn to shiver. And it wasn't from fear. "Fine." She gestured at the wolfman. "Have at him. But call your sister first. And maybe the pack in Colorado so they can start making their way west."

"You guys really know how to do date night," Bill commented, sounding very *not* scared anymore.

"We really don't," Cary said.

4

$\mathcal{N}$either she nor Deacon had charged outside with their coats. And he mostly wore his for show rather than any real need. Along with burning off all the food he ate so he never had to worry about weight—the bastard—his shifter metabolism kept him warmer than humans in cold weather.

Cary was not feeling so warm by the time Deacon finished his calls.

"You're shivering," he said as he handed her his cellphone to keep safe.

Then to her surprise, he stripped off his shirt and handed it to her.

"Uh," she mumbled, taking it. She'd lost the powers of speech at the sight of his magnificent chest.

"I know it's not as thick as a coat," he said, his gaze on the wolf-man, "but it'll help a little. It's going to take Cate a few minutes to get here."

The shirt was still warm from his body. And it smelled like him. And she could easily wrap herself up in this piece of material for the rest of her life and be content. She breathed in deeply as she slipped her arms through the sleeves.

23

"You sure you don't want to just wait for Caitlin?" she asked him, her gaze also on the panting, salivating wolfman.

He hadn't paused in his attack for even a moment. He was accumulating cuts all over his body, and blood matted in the patches of fur that kept appearing and disappearing. Where there was human skin, the damage was more obvious. All self-inflicted from hitting the tarmac or the fence or the trash bins. And once he'd managed to get thrown inside the giant bin.

They were just lucky no one had come out to investigate the noise yet.

"Where are your colleagues?" she asked Bill, realizing someone *should* have come looking for him by now. And also that she hadn't seen the ticket collector inside when she'd come out.

"Sarah is on a break—she sneaks up to one of the projector rooms to make out with Kumar when she's on a break. And Edna sticks to the ticket booth without paying much attention to what's happening inside. She watches her 'stories' on her phone when there's nothing going on."

"Cool. Cool." Two less people to worry about. "No one else I need to watch out for?" she asked.

Deacon rolled his head, his neck cracking a little, and rolled his shoulders to loosen them up as he watched for an opening in the wolfman's attack.

"The manager is sick tonight," Bill said, "so he's hiding in the back office. Claims he doesn't want patrons to see him sniffling, in case they worry about the food."

Cary shrugged. "Probably a good idea." She'd wonder about the popcorn if she saw one of the employees sneezing too near the concessions stand. "That's it?"

"Only other people working tonight are running the projectors or the cleaning staff and they hang out in the cleaning supplies room while the theaters are full. No idea what they do there."

Cary choose not to speculate either.

The wolfman charged and bounced off her shield again, this time getting tossed back into the fence so hard he paused a moment, shaking his head. Deacon used that brief moment of disorientation to attack. He moved at shifter speeds, since only Bill was there to witness, and had the giant wolfman in a neck lock before Cary realized he was no longer behind her.

Bill gasped. "How did he do that?"

She tried to wave it away. "He's pretty fit."

"He is," Bill said quietly. "Your boyfriend's super handsome."

She blinked a few times at someone calling Deacon her boyfriend. She still stumbled over the word herself.

"How'd he end up with you?"

She scowled back over her shoulder. "That's pretty insulting, Bill. Especially when I'm saving your life."

"Sorry." His eyes had gone wide. "I didn't mean it that way. Just wondering how you two met."

Right. "Long story," she said, still scowling as she faced forward again.

Unfortunately for Bill, he'd hit on one of her insecurities. She still often wondered what Deacon was doing with her. And if it hadn't been for the mate thing, the chemical reaction he couldn't really help, would he have given her a second glance.

The fact that someone besides her wondered about them being together did not help with that particular insecurity.

The wolfman struggled against Deacon's hold, scratching at his arms. While the wolfman's wounds were healing, slowly but still faster than a human would, Deacon healed at regular shifter speeds—which was to say really fast. No sooner had he been injured than the injury started to seal closed. A relief for her because the wolfman's claws were not small.

"You okay?" she called.

"Fine," Deacon grunted. "Stop that," he hissed at the struggling wolf who'd raked him with his claws again.

The wolfman climbed to his feet, dragging Deacon up with him, a show of strength that made her eyes widen. Despite having Deacon still hanging off his neck, which had to be choking him, the wolfman lunged forward a few staggering steps. Then he spun and slammed Deacon against the big trash bin.

Cary winced. "Still okay?"

"Fine," Deacon said, his voice a little more strained now.

"Why isn't he choking and collapsing?" she asked quietly, mostly to herself.

"Fucking thick neck," Deacon answered through gritted teeth.

She shook her head. Shifter hearing.

The wolfman slammed Deacon into the trash bin again. Deacon hissed another curse. Then he set his feet against the bin and used it for leverage to push himself and the wolfman away from it. He pushed hard enough the wolfman went sprawling forward, landing on his stomach, with Deacon on his back.

"Oh, good move!" Cary gave the air a little punch.

"When did you two meet?" Bill asked. He sounded a bit more wistful than curious.

The fact that this was still a topic was a little irritating. And she really didn't want to admit out loud to a stranger that she and Deacon had only known each other a few months.

"One Halloween," she said vaguely, hoping he didn't realize she meant just this last Halloween. "Black cats and stuff."

And boy was that an understatement of their first meeting.

The wolfman pushed up onto his hands and knees, despite Deacon's weight. Deacon was still clinging to his back, his arm wrapped tightly around the wolf's neck. The wolfman was starting to turn very red where she could see skin around the patches of fur. But he just kept moving.

With a choked howl, he flipped over and landed on Deacon, reversing their positions. Deacon grunted. Cary winced again. The fact that his grip hadn't loosened enough for wolfman to get away was a testament to his determination.

But…he didn't look in the best position to win this fight anymore.

"Need any help?" she called.

"Nope. Got it."

It seemed disloyal to point out that he didn't look like he had this.

"How long has it been since he called his sister?" she asked Bill, hoping he had a watch of some kind. She was afraid to look away from the fight to check her phone—which she realized was still in the theater in her coat pocket along with her wallet and her house keys. She sighed. Hopefully, no one stole the coat while she was out here.

Maybe she *should* have worn one of Marianne's skirts or pants since her friend always put in magic pockets. Though, to be fair, a leather miniskirt would have been over the top for a movie and dinner. And she wasn't sure pockets would have made up for that. Also, really, she hadn't intended to be doing her job in the middle of a date.

"It's been about fifteen minutes," Bill said, brandishing his cellphone in front of her.

"Thanks." She paused. "You're not…taking pictures or video are you? Cause, that's not going to be good."

"Shit. I forgot."

"Don't start now! I will smash that phone, Bill, without even a second of remorse."

Bill gulped visibly at her glare and tucked his phone back into his pocket.

"Better." She faced Deacon again. Cellphones were great until you wanted to keep some supernatural mischief from finding its way onto the internet. Then things got less great.

She half wondered how the Nags and all the other supernatural types sorted out the whole everything-is-recorded-on-cellphones thing. Probably something she should ask someone about.

Deacon roared, sounding, to her relief, more angry and irritated than hurt. He somehow managed to get his legs wedged under the larger man's body and pushed up. And because Deacon was a super strong shifter, the move sent the wolfman flying.

He slammed face first into the trash bin and slid to the ground like something from a comic book.

Deacon climbed to his feet, his eyes glowing yellow, his brows lowered, his mouth tight. He looked very very angry now. Which really, she shouldn't have found sexy.

This mate thing was turning her into a sex fiend.

Deacon charged the wolfman before he could move, the speed of the attack blurring both him and the wolfman.

"He's not…human, is he?" Bill asked.

"Why would you say that?" Cary said, not looking Bill. "Beyond the wolf snout and claws. I guess those really do sort of give it away, don't they?"

"I meant your boyfriend," Bill said.

"Oh."

"Are you going to tell me what he is?"

"What who is, Bill?" She gasped as the wolfman got in a lucky shot and punched Deacon in the jaw. Then she looked at Bill and raised her brows, as deadpan as possible.

Bill looked at her, looked at the fight, looked back at her. "Never mind."

"Good decision," she said.

Deacon grunted and she spun to see the wolfman getting in another solid punch, this one to Deacon's gut.

"Want a break?" she called. "I could step in, keep everyone separated for a few minutes?"

"No," Deacon said, rubbing his stomach. "I'm good."

He grinned in a way that made Cary raise her brows. He was having fun now? She shook her head. Men.

The two shifters jumped at each other and the fight blurred again. Mostly Deacon's movements were blurred. She realized the wolfman, for all his size and strength, wasn't nearly as fast as Deacon. He might technically be a shifter, but he definitely didn't have the hang of his shifter abilities.

She rolled her eyes. The partial shift really should have clued her in. Her only excuse for not realizing that sooner was that she was worried about Deacon.

Which she shouldn't have been.

He lifted the wolfman up over his head in a move that reminded her of a wrestling match and dropped him hard onto the concrete.

"Ouch," Bill said.

"Yeah," Cary agreed.

The wolfman didn't move for a long moment, just lay there groaning.

"You guys all done?" she asked.

"We'll see." Deacon stood a few feet from the prone man, hands on his hips, and waited. He was safely out of range of the other shifter's longer reach, but close enough to engage again if the wolfman decided to stand up.

"I leave you alone for a couple of months and this is what happens?" a new voice said from the other side of the chainlink fence.

A stunning woman with dark brown hair and brown eyes that were just a little gold stood there shaking her head at Deacon. She was a little taller than Cary, though not as tall as Deacon, slim, and dressed in a beautifully tailored indigo pants suit that Marianne would have approved. Her tanned skin tone was just a little paler than Deacon's, her lips a bit fuller, but her eye were almost identical.

The family resemblance was unmistakable.

"Cate," Deacon greeted with a smile. "Cary, this is my sister Caitlin Jones. Cate, Cary Redmond."

Caitlin's smile widened. "It is a real pleasure to *finally* meet you, Cary Redmond. I think we have a lot to talk about."

Oh boy.

5

"*D*id you bring the tranquilizer?" Deacon asked, breaking into Cary's momentary panic.

Caitlin raised a little metal case.

"Then get over here and—"

His sentence cut off when the wolfman lunged and grabbed him by his leg, tossing him to the ground.

There was a collective gasp. Deacon rolled to the side before the wolfman got to his neck, but then the fight blurred again and Cary couldn't tell who was winning.

Caitlin spoke from beside her, which made both Cary and Bill jump. Damned shifter speed.

"He'll be fine," she said, nodding at Deacon. "The exercise is good for him."

"Exercise? Sure." Cary blinked at her mate's sister.

Caitlin was one of Deacon's six sisters, younger than him by about ten years, though all of them were older than they looked thanks to the way shifters aged differently to humans. He had eight brothers as well. A big family that included a twin sister, who lived on the east coast, and a twin brother down near Eugene.

The fact that there were two people in the world as gorgeous as

Deacon had always made Cary's head spin. And apparently, the family tendency toward gorgeousness didn't extend just to his twins.

"When this is over, you want to get a coffee?" Caitlin asked. "Deacon's been saying he'll introduce us and then stalling, so I suspect we have *tons* to talk about."

"Uh." Words? What were those?

"Who're you?" Bill asked.

Caitlin gave him a look. "Who are you?"

"Bill," Bill said. "I work here."

"We're saving him from the wolfman," Cary offered.

"Ah. Hi, Bill. I'm Caitlin. Deacon's sister," Caitlin said, repeating the earlier introduction.

Which seemed redundant, but given Bill's expression maybe he'd missed the earlier part of the conversation. His eyes were rounded little saucers, and he looked like he'd been hit with a board again.

"Okay," he said.

To be fair to Bill, Caitlin was so outrageously stunning, Cary was having trouble processing it, too.

"Is your whole family gorgeous?" Cary asked.

"Ah, aren't you sweet," Caitlin said. "Thank you. You'll have to meet the rest of the family and tell me." She winked.

"Uh."

"Stop scaring my mate, Caitlin," Deacon called. He had the wolfman in a choke hold again, the larger man bent backward nearly in half as Deacon tried to keep him still.

"Didn't know I was," Caitlin said pleasantly. "You ready for the tranquilizer yet or still want to play some more?"

Deacon grunted. "Ready."

Caitlin bent and opened the little metal box, taking out two syringes.

"Two?" Cary asked.

Caitlin studied the positions of the two fighters as she answered. "This one is the elephant tranquilizer." She lifted the syringe in her right hand. "This one is a mix our younger sister's been working on."

She lifted the syringe in her left hand. "Just a tiny touch of silver in it to help weaken werewolves."

"That come in handy much?" Cary asked. "In the animal rescue business."

"You'd be surprised." Caitlin darted forward.

She moved at shifter speed so Cary didn't see the syringes going in. Just a blur of movement and Caitlin jumping backward out of the wolfman's reach. The drugs took effect almost instantly, the wolfman's body lunging sideways as he weakened. He kept trying to claw at Deacon's arm around his neck, and he stumbled a few times trying to right himself, but the fight didn't last long. He collapsed in a heap that brought Deacon to his knees, arm still around the larger man's neck.

"Well." Deacon glanced up at Cary and smiled. "That was fun."

She snorted. "You hurt?"

"Nothing that won't heal."

She spotted the blood on his arms and chest, and had to assume some of it was his, but she couldn't see any remaining open wounds. Just a few red welts were an injury had been.

Thanks to the Protector magic Cary channeled, she healed fast now, too. But nothing like a shifter, and frankly, she was envious. It took her a good twenty-four hours to heal from broken ribs. Serious wounds, it depended but anywhere from hours to days. Her medical record was an appalling collection of weird injuries that ensured all doctors looked at her like she needed help.

"What should we do with him?" Cary asked, nodding at the now unconscious wolfman. "He's still breathing right?"

"Still breathing," Deacon confirmed. He glanced at Caitlin. "We have a cage that will hold him?"

"Sure. We can use the one at the Laurelhurst facility that we use for the big animals. Should hold him for a day or so if we give him a booster shot of Julia's concoction. When's the werewolf due to arrive?"

"Tomorrow, midday," Deacon said, climbing back to his feet and letting the wolfman slump onto the cement. "The pack is sending their beta."

"Help me get him into the back of the van," Caitlin said, returning the now empty syringes to the small metal case. "I'll take care of him from there."

"You sure you won't need help?" Cary asked, giving the huge man a look. Shifters were exceptionally strong, but…well, the guy was really big.

"I have staff at the facility that can help," Caitlin said. "I can take care of him on my own, but I have to keep up the illusion of being human for our employees. Especially after Deacon almost gave away the game."

Deacon winced at the reminder. "Let's not talk about that." He nodded at Bill.

Cary winced a little, too. Not long after they'd met, Deacon's control had been so bad he'd had an incident at work. Caitlin hadn't let him come back to work since.

"Wait, one question," Cary said, pointing to the downed man. "He still looks half wolf."

They all looked at the unconscious man. The tranquilizer had stopped the racing of fur in and out, leaving patches of skin interspersed with patches of fur. There was no mad dance of undecided shifting going on anymore, but he hadn't fallen into one form or the other, either. He was still, very clearly, half wolf, half man.

"You sure you want to expose humans to that?" she asked. "They're going to ask questions."

"Yeah, like why do you keep referring to 'humans' like you all are different?" Bill said.

"Bill." Cary turned to face him. "We just saved your life. Do you really want to pull that string and unravel the blanket of your reality? Or maybe, just maybe, you think, 'hey, some really nice people helped save me from a mugger-murderer and I'm going to thank them by keeping my mouth shut.' What do you think, Bill?"

"I think I'm grateful not to be dead so I'm gonna keep my mouth shut," Bill said.

Cary smiled at him. "I knew I liked you. You're a good man. And I'm glad we saved your life." She paused. "Or maybe just saved you from becoming like him."

Bill visibly shuddered.

"Cary raises a good point," Deacon said to Caitlin. "You can't have other humans around him."

Caitlin made a face. "I was hoping the silver would help with that. Poor bastard."

"The Colorado beta should be able to help him," Deacon said quietly.

Cary could only imagine how they felt seeing someone half shifted. They *couldn't* get stuck, but still it must get into their heads sometimes.

This was one of those moments she was really grateful to be a human, and an ordinary one at that. Except for the Protector magic she channeled, there was nothing supernatural or preternatural about her. In her world, that could sometimes be a bad thing. Right now, it was a relief.

Caitlin put her hands on her hips and shook her head. "I'll have to call ahead and send the night crew home and just handle everything at the facility until the wolf beta gets here. Or we'll have to store him somewhere else. Short of driving him all the way to Eugene and putting him into lockdown with mother..."

Deacon's expression lightened at that. "Don't want to pay her a visit?"

"Right now? With the charity ball coming up? No, thank you. I'll get roped into staying and doing work for her. I have more than enough to do here with you..." She waved a hand in the air. "Incapacitated."

Deacon winced. "Your choice what to do with him."

Caitlin glanced between Cary and Deacon. "I can haul him around and get him into a cage on my own. The problem is looking after the rest of the facility until the wolf beta arrives. If he's not there before the day crew shows up, I'll have to get them to come in late... It's going to be complicated and there will be questions."

"Could you tell your employees something toxic got released in the facility?" Bill suggested.

Cary glanced at him. "You're helping?"

"You saved my life." He shrugged. When he glanced at the wolf-man, he shuddered again. "Or saved me from something worse."

Cary patted his arm. "Thank you."

"I hate to ask," Caitlin said, "because I know you're on a date, but Deacon, can you keep it together long enough to help me until the wolf arrives?"

"I could go with you," Cary said. Her presence helped Deacon stay in better control of his leopard. Not exactly a convenient aspect to the mate thing, but not a lot they could do about it either.

Deacon groaned. "Not the way I meant for this night to go," he said to her.

"We tried." Her stomach growled, loudly, and her cheeks heated. "Do you think we can order a pizza or something once we've settled this guy? I'm kind of hungry now."

"You don't like anything weird on your pizzas, do you?" Caitlin asked. "Like pineapple?"

"No," Cary said very firmly. "No pineapple on pizza."

"I knew I'd like you," Caitlin said with a grin.

"My sister and my mate bonding over pizza." Deacon closed his eyes. "This isn't going to end well for me, is it?"

Caitlin laughed and pointed at her brother. "Help me get this guy into the van. Cary, can you…finish things up here?" She nodded at Bill.

"I have to go grab my jacket too," Cary said. "I'll be back out in a minute."

She escorted Bill back inside as Deacon lifted the wolfman and flung him over his shoulder. Since the unconscious man was bleeding, that was very nice of him, keeping his sister's suit from getting dirty.

Bill promised not to tell anyone about what had happened, mostly because he didn't want to get accused of being high and get fired. Since he'd gone out behind the building to get high, this was a real concern for him.

No one had stolen her coat, thankfully, but the movie was half over. She sighed. They could try seeing it again. Maybe not at this particular movie theater… But still, they could try all this again.

So much for their first date.

And she'd been worried they wouldn't have anything to talk about.

DATE NIGHT TAKE TWO

If at first you don't succeed...

Cary Redmond's first attempt at a real date with her leopard shifter mate definitely did not go according to plan. In fact, the date went so disastrously wrong, they decide to try again. Clean slate. Another movie. Another dinner reservation.

Another interruption she can't ignore.

Wizard and vampire fights wait for no woman. And as Portland's resident magical Protector, Cary has to answer the call of someone in danger. No matter the cost.

1

ary climbed out of Deacon's SUV, smoothing down her skirt, her heartbeat thudding hard as she glanced at him over the car's hood. Deacon Jones looked almost painfully handsome in his simple dress shirt and slacks, a black wool coat over the whole thing as a nod to the winter weather even though his shifter metabolism meant he didn't really need the extra layer. His black hair was combed neatly, but he needed a haircut. His golden eyes sparkled with a sensual knowledge that made her pulse pound.

It didn't seem to matter that she saw him all the time, and they spent most nights together, she still got breathless at the oddest moments when looking at him.

This was one of those moments. Their second attempt at a first date.

No man should look so stunningly gorgeous just glancing at you over the hood of a car.

He smiled.

She melted.

When she could collect herself from the puddle she'd become on the concrete floor, she pulled her coat tighter around her. Her little black dress was beautiful, and flattering if she did say so herself, but it was made for pretty, not warm. And Cary didn't have a shifter metabolism. In fact, at that very moment, she was just an ordinary human woman, attempting a date with a man who had decided she was his mate and had stuck by her ever since—despite some of the pretty scary jobs she'd had to do recently.

Her job as a magical Protector for the greater Portland, Oregon area had a habit of keeping her busy. And interfering with their developing romantic life.

The first time they'd tried a date had… Well, it had started fine. Until the whole werewolf thing had interrupted them. A week later, with the city alight in holiday frivolity, they were trying this again.

She'd needed the week to do some minor jobs for her bosses, who had a habit of popping up all the time to demand she run off and protect someone. Since she got paid to do that, she couldn't exactly say no. And to make matters worse, she was in the first month of a test year, a year when she had to do all this on her own without the help of her mentor, and that made refusing jobs impossible. Even if she wanted to.

Which, to be honest, she usually didn't. She might not like how she got tricked into being a Protector, but it was a useful skill to have when, say a bad guy was trying to rip out the throat of a poor movie theater concessions clerk just trying to grab a smoke.

"Think we'll make it through the movie tonight?" Deacon asked.

The rumble of his deep voice made her toes curl. She tried not to wobble in her high heels as she walked around the car to meet him. They'd picked a parking lot downtown that was near enough to both a movie theater and the restaurant he'd gotten reservations at for later. It was all very…date-like. And for some reason, the formality of it all had her nerves hopping.

Or maybe that was Deacon's smile.

"I hope so," she said, trying—and failing miserably—to be casual. "I really really want to see this."

His smile widened. "You're nervous again."

"Stop reading my mind." She scowled.

He tapped his nose. "I can't really help it."

Damned shifter sense of smell. "Things didn't go exactly to plan last time."

"Uh huh," he murmured.

"What?" she snapped.

"I literally just left your bed this morning. And you're still nervous about a *date*, even though we've barely left each other's company for the last two months?"

"The last time we tried this, things went very wrong. Of course, I'm nervous."

"You met my sister. That was good. For you two."

Cary grinned at that. She did like Deacon's younger sister, Caitlin. She especially liked the way Caitlin gave her big brother shit without fear. "She's called and asked, again, if we can meet for coffee sometime, you know."

"Shit."

She laughed at the resignation in his expression, and some of her jumping anxiety eased. This was Deacon. He was right. She'd seen him naked—just that morning. She really had no reason to be nervous just because they were on an official date.

Now if she could just pull herself together after the thought of Deacon naked turned her into a giant lust puddle, she'd be fine.

But when they stepped out of the garage and onto the city sidewalk, the sweep of awareness through her system destroyed any sense of ease she'd managed.

She turned with a resigned sigh to face her bosses.

_L_iruk and Wisat rarely popped up in the middle of a city sidewalk to disrupt her life. They usually confined themselves to more private places to give her her assignments and generally be a pain in her ass.

Despite materializing in the middle of the city, on a side street that should have had plenty of pedestrian traffic this time of the evening, they hadn't bothered to change their appearance. From the lack of people walking by, Cary assumed they'd done some Fae mojo to keep the innocent bystanders away.

Probably for the best if they weren't going to even make an attempt to blend in with their surroundings. The mundane humans would probably lose their minds if they beheld the Nags. There was no way to write them off as anything but supernatural.

They were eerily beautiful but in a way that wasn't like ordinary ideas of beauty. It was like looking at the exquisite landscape of an alien planet. Stunning in a way that was hard for the brain to comprehend. Some Fae were just that way. And Cary suspected the Nags toned themselves down when they appeared for her. Which made their appearances even more overwhelming.

Wisat was all black and red, black robe, black hair, red skin, the velvet-covered antler halo circling his head also red. And his green green eyes like glowing jewels. Liruk was white and gold, white hair that hung almost to the ground, white robe, twin little golden horns poking out of her hair, and skin a color of light brown that glowed like gold. Her green eyes matched Wisat's, a particular feature of their Fae nature or coincidence she wasn't sure. And she'd never been brave enough to ask.

"What?" she snapped. "We're on a date."

Wisat nodded to Deacon in greeting.

Liruk ignored him. "You are required immediately, Protector," she said without preamble—or any discernable regret for disrupting Cary's date. "If you do not get between the wizard and the vampire, there will be grave consequences for the city."

Her shoulders dropped with her sigh. "Where are they?" She frowned. "And which one am I protecting?"

"The wizard. In this particular case," Wisat said.

"Oh good." There was no little sarcasm in her tone. She'd had trouble with both vampires and wizards in the last few months. And there was a wizard running around trying to kill her. So she was a little punchy about both.

But at least there wasn't a demon involved. She'd be happy if she never had to deal with another demon again.

"Where?" she repeated.

The Nags sent her to a location not too far from the parking garage, out behind one of the larger nightclubs just outside the Pearl. It was early enough in the night that the nightclub wasn't particularly busy yet, but there were still people passing by on the street out front and the music from the nightclub filtered out into the back.

The stench of garbage waiting to be collected made her wince for Deacon's sake. Her ordinary human senses weren't keen on the smell. His super shifter senses probably hated places like this. Or maybe not? She'd have to ask him. Maybe shifters didn't mind the stench of garbage because they were used to everything having a strong smell?

Huh?

She redirected her wandering thoughts to the two people standing near the back of the nightclub's two story brick façade. Colorful graffiti gave the place a suitably city appearance, though the artwork was top class which meant the owners had probably commissioned it. A metal fire escape balcony and ladder hung over the heads of the two men, and a black bird of some kind sat on the railing watching the standoff.

That was…weird.

Deacon murmured in her ear, "That's not the wizard trying to kill you?"

"Nope," she said. "Too young. Unless he's a shapeshifter, too."

"He's not."

"Then we should be good. Doubt the Nags would have sent me to protect the wizard trying to kill me."

Deacon didn't comment on that last part. She couldn't blame him.

"You want my help?" he whispered.

She tried not to notice the feel of his breath against her cheek. Warm and sexy… And wow, she'd rather be on their date than working.

"I've got this," she said. "But…uhm, stay out of the way of any errant wizard bolts. If things get hairy, get close so I can protect you, too."

She felt his nod against her cheek. "I'm here if you need me, but I don't want to make things worse by aggravating the vampire. I'll blend into the shadows."

"He'll still know you're there."

"He's too focused on the wizard to be worried about me. He'll ignore me if I don't get involved."

"Cool." She handed Deacon her purse. Why she'd thought carrying a purse was a good idea she'd never know. She'd given up carrying purses early on in her Protector career because they just got in the way. Or she dropped and lost then. But this was supposed to be a date.

She sighed and trotted toward the two youngish men facing each other, both of them glaring. She kicked into a full run, regretting her heels immediately, when the vampire lunged at the wizard and the wizard raised an energy bolt on the palm of his hand.

The physical act of getting between two powerful beings about to pummel each other was always a little risky. Doing it in heels gave her a whole new appreciation for those old school actresses who could dance their way through any situation in heels and still come out looking elegant.

Cary's slide and scramble and twisted ankle were not in any way elegant. And breaking one high heel in the process just added insult to injury.

"Okay, okay," she said, raising her hands to chest level on both men. "Everyone is going to calm down right now."

Though she was technically here to save the wizard, she wasn't in a hurry to put her back to him. Standing sideways between them still initiated her Protector powers but meant she could keep an eye on both her charge and the vampire. Just in case.

The wizard looked a bit on the young side, early twenties maybe, pale skin, dark hair, brown eyes that would have been really striking if he wasn't glaring daggers at the vampire. He was as tall as her in her heels which made him close to, or right on six foot tall. And he was dressed for the cold in a thick ski jacket and hiking boots that looked well worn, though it was hard to tell in the dark. They only had a little illumination from the overhead security light above the fire escape.

The vampire was taller, maybe Deacon's height or more, and was not dressed for the cold. He wore a tailored suit of some dark silk material that gave it a weird shiny texture. Rather than a tie, he had a vest beneath the fitted coat, same material as the suit. The white shirt beneath the vest blended with his preternaturally pale skin. His dark hair was short and smoothed back from his face, a style that high-lighted his long jawline and the sharp cut of his cheekbones.

He returned the wizard's dagger-eyed stare, only his eyes glowed yellow. And his dangerously pointy canines showed from between his snarling lips.

She had enough experience with vampires and wizards to realize that they were both potentially deadly, and only a very stupid person would get in between them.

"No fighting this early in the evening when there are so many people out in front of this club," she said. Honestly, there weren't that many people. But there would be in another few hours. She was just fudging the timeline a little.

"He owes the Master," the vampire hissed. "He will pay."

"I don't owe him shit," the wizard spat. "You can tell Gabriel to fuck off."

Cary sighed. Why was she here? This seemed like something the wizard and the vampires could sort out for themselves. Why would the Nags send her to protect a wizard who would get in bad with the Master of Portland? She personally tried to *avoid* Gabriel at all costs. She'd managed to swim under his radar and not drawn his attention since he took over the city. She'd prefer to keep it that way.

But this was her job, so she supposed she'd better do it. "No fighting. No payments. No chaos. You two should know better. If you wanted to fight, you should have taken it somewhere private, where no mundane humans could get hurt."

There was a brief pause. Then both men looked at her as if seeing her for the first time.

"What?" she asked.

"Who are you?" the wizard asked.

"What are you?" the vampire said. "I can't read your mind."

"Well, that's good to know," she said sternly. "And I'm just a concerned citizen, trying to prevent you two bozos from bringing down the house." She nodded to the brick building at her back. "In a bad way."

It occurred to her that that might very well be why the Nags had sent her. Two powerful beings having a pissing match at the back of a nightclub—even a half empty one—could be a disaster and cost more than one life.

But if that were the case, why not just tell her?

"This is none of your business," the vampire said, his glowing eyes turning back to the wizard. "He offered his blood in exchange for Gabriel's help. He must pay."

"I'm not letting *you* suck my blood," the wizard hissed. "I made that offer to Gabriel."

"I'm one of his. He offered his reward to me."

"No." Cary stomped her foot, the one with the broken heel so she wobbled a little on her one still intact shoe. "No. No. No unwilling victims. That's the rule."

The vampire scowled at her again. "How do you know the rules of the hive?"

She'd actually had a hand in that rule being established with the previous Master of Portland. Because vampires shouldn't go around sucking innocent kitten blood. It was just wrong on too many levels. When Gabriel had overthrown Ariel, he'd agreed to uphold all her laws —which meant that in Portland, vampires *only* took from willing victims.

But she wasn't sure admitting to the strange vampire that she was the one who'd gotten Ariel to agree to that law was a wise idea. So she just said, "You hear things." She gestured to the wizard. "Offering to feed one vampire does not convey consent to all vampires. That's not how consent works."

"The Master is not to be crossed," the vampire said, his glowing eyes narrowed.

"I'm not crossing the Master," she said, as if that was obvious. "I'm crossing you. And you I can deal with."

He lifted his lip in a faint, teeth-revealing snarl. "You think you can stop one of my power?"

She sighed. "Boy, you guys are predictable. New. Dialogue. Please."

The wizard chuckled.

She pointed at him. "Don't you get cocky here. You made a deal with a vampire Master. I'm not counting you one of the good guys yet either."

"I only offered him my blood so I could get..." He snapped his mouth shut and looked away.

Cary gestured for him to continue. "You might as well tell me. I'm not going anywhere until this is finished. And if you want it finished without the vampires coming after you again, I need to know what's up."

That wasn't technically true. There was nothing she could do about the vampires coming after him again except continuing to get between him and them. But she was curious. And nosey. And she really wanted to know why the Nags had sent her to protect him.

"I can take care of the vampires who try me," the wizard said.

Cary sighed. She'd hoped for the good gossip. Oh well. "Fine. You want to keep fighting and testing who has the biggest d_ck I can't stop you. But I can stop you here and now because there are innocent humans walking around. And I will not have them getting hurt by stray wizard bolts and rampaging vampires."

"Again, I'd like to know what makes you think you can stop us," the vampire said.

She noticed he didn't comment on their fight being a biggest-dick contest. "I'm very good at stopping bad guys from hurting good guys."

"Thought you didn't consider me a good guy," the wizard said.

"Don't pout. You made a deal with a vampire Master."

"If you think your shifter will save you," the vampire said, "you're wrong."

Cary rolled her eyes. "Of *course* you think I'd need a man to save me. I will have you know, I'm the one here doing the saving. He's staying out of the way so I don't have to save *him*. So you can just fuck off with your sexism, thank you very much."

The vampire glared at her. She glared back.

The vampire blinked very slowly and said, "He's a *shifter*. You are a human. It's not sexism."

"Speciesism then." Was that a word? "Anyway, that's not the point. The point is, we were supposed to be on a date until you bozos disrupted that with your pissing match. And I'm not very happy about that interruption. Which means I'm not in the mood to deal with your nonsense. Go away. Leave the wizard alone. If Gabriel wants to suck his blood, well then *Gabriel* and Gabriel alone is allowed since he made the deal."

She glanced at the wizard. "I still want to know what the hell motivated you to do something so boneheaded. Really? A deal with the vampire Master?" She tisked.

The wizard winced and frowned down at the ground.

Without warning, the vampire lunged. Cary sighed as he was tossed backward onto his ass by her shield. "Well that was a dumbass idea, now, wasn't it? Did you hurt yourself?"

The vampire roared and charged her, claws out. Literally claws out since he had his fingernails shaped into long, sharp points at the ends of his very very pale, skeletal fingers. Obviously, he hadn't eaten in a while. There was no "meat" on his bones, so to speak.

That was interesting.

She took a closer look at the vampire as he bounced off her shield again.

His elegant, if shiny, suit hid the fact that he was pretty thin underneath. And now that she considered him closer, his high cheekbones looked less like a natural feature and more like his cheeks were so sunken and hollow that his bones were poking through. With his mouth open, flashing those wicked sharp teeth as he bounced off her magic for the third time, he looked every inch the retched, skeletal vampire of old. Not the beautifully elegant image they—and to be fair, popular culture—portrayed, but like he was wasting away.

Someone hadn't had a meal in much much too long. And that made this particular vampire infinitely more dangerous than she'd assumed.

Since she'd assumed he was pretty dangerous, this was not a welcomed realization.

3

"Why haven't you fed?" Cary asked the vampire in between attempts to charge her, as he panted and glared. The overhead security light yellowed his white skin, adding a sickly cast to his emaciated complexion.

"What makes you think I haven't?" he snapped.

"You look like shit. And every vampire I've ever met is too vain to show up looking like shit unless they don't have the energy for projecting gorgeousness."

The vampire snarled at her, his lips pulled back to reveal his sharp canines more obviously. From the shadows in Deacon's general direction, she thought she heard him growl in response. But he didn't come loping in to get himself into trouble and for that she was grateful.

She imagined it was kind of tough on a shifter to watch his mate in potential danger and just stand back and wait. Seemed to her that went against the grain for most of them. The fact that Deacon tried to curb his instincts when she did her job was pretty nice. She felt a little smile rising at the idea and had to flatten her lips. The vampire wouldn't understand the smile.

"My feeding habits are none of your concern, woman," the vampire said.

"Sure sure. Just wondering. You guys get dangerous when you don't feed. Anyway." She looked back at the wizard as the vampire lunged at her again. "Why did you get yourself into this mess? And why the fight here in the middle of things? And will you please put that wizard bolt away." She nodded to the ball of blue-green energy he held in his hand as he glared at the vampire. "You're gonna hurt someone with that."

"That's the idea," he said.

"Put. The. Bolt. Away." She carefully enunciated each word. "You could hurt an innocent bystander."

"He'll just keep coming," the wizard said. "Don't want them to think I'm a pushover."

"Yeah, yeah, I know. The dick measuring hasn't stopped yet. But you'll have to put it away for now because I'm not allowing any fights —" she turned and pointedly looked at the vampire, "—or feedings right now." She faced the wizard again. Who, she noted sourly, had *not* given up his wizard bolt yet. "What's your name and why are we here?"

"None of your business. On both counts."

She rolled her eyes. Most of the time, the person she was protecting was scared and open for a little conversation. They were usually happy when she got in the way of the bad guy. This whole mess felt like she was standing in the middle of *two* bad guys to prevent a fight and that was just irritating. She was supposed to be on a date right now. Seeing a fun superhero movie. Eating a nice dinner. Trying not to combust every time Deacon smiled at her.

This current situation was *not* her idea of fun.

Also, she wasn't sure how to make the two assholes stop, and she couldn't get back to her date until they did.

"What will it take to get the two of you to end this and go your separate ways?" she asked. Sometimes a woman had to take the blunt approach.

"Gabriel gave this insect to me," the vampire said, his lip lifted. It cracked with the gesture, but no blood eased through.

That wasn't good. The guy really was starving. That made him a whole hell of a lot more unpredictable.

"Why?" she asked, again with the bluntness. "Why you? Why this guy? Why all this?"

"None of your business."

Argh! "Fine. You guys don't want to tell me what's going on, fine. But I'm not going anywhere until this ends. And while I'd rather be on my date, I can stand here all night if I have to. At which point, you—" she pointed at the vampire, "—will be too weak to carry on this fight. Even if you were well fed."

Vampires could walk around in the daylight just fine without turning to dust or anything. But they were photosensitive and had to wear sunglasses, even in the cloudy Pacific Northwest. And they got very weak. Human-level weak. Since no vampire she knew of liked that feeling, they mostly only came out at night.

Another worry occurred to her, though. If the guy was starving, he might leave the wizard but still go off and drain some poor innocent victim because he couldn't control his hunger.

Why the hell had Gabriel allowed one of his vampires to get to this state? It was dangerous. For the entire hive. One starved and desperate vampire could go on a killing spree that brought unwanted attention and threat to all of them. It was the Master's responsibility to prevent that kind of thing. Was Gabriel *trying* to cause trouble for his people?

The absolute worst thing, though… Neither of these guys was inclined to do the bad-guy-monologuing and spill the beans on what was happening. She hated that. Bad guy monologues were a really useful source of information if she could get them talking. And she was usually able to aggravate them enough that they did end up talking. She had a gift for irritating dangerous people.

That probably wasn't a good thing.

"I will feed," the vampire said. "I have waited long enough. And his power will restore me."

Well that was a hint at least, though she still didn't have a clue why any vampire in their right mind would "wait" to feed until they got this desperate.

"I am not your food," the wizard said, his eyes narrowing. The wizard bolt of energy swirling in a little glowing orb on his palm pulsed and grew slightly in size.

"Would you two stop already," she snapped. "I'm not letting you feed. I'm not letting you—"

She cut off abruptly when the wizard snarled and threw his energy bolt at the vampire. The bolt hit Cary's shield and scattered over it, the blue-green light breaking apart like water. Apparently, she was protecting them both from each other.

"Hey," she snapped at the wizard. "That was rude."

"Get out of my way," he said, his voice low and deep.

"No. And if you don't stop, you're going to get hurt."

"How?" he asked as another ball of energy swirled to life on his open palm.

"My boyfriend is going to stop being so patient."

She'd heard Deacon's hiss when the wizard threw the bolt. While he might know in his gut she was fine, that didn't always ease his leopard's instincts. And his leopard had a habit of jumping in the middle of these things to try and keep her safe even when Deacon trusted her enough to do her job.

Frankly, that was sometimes useful because then she could protect Deacon and then they were both safe.

Still, she'd prefer he didn't get in the middle of all this. Not when his control was still so…well, not really there. The last thing she needed was to have to protect the assholes from her own boyfriend, while protecting the assholes from each other, *and* protecting Deacon from stray wizard bolts and vampire attacks.

She'd broken ribs protecting Deacon from a wizard attack once before. She'd rather not do that tonight. She'd hate having to go to the hospital in her pretty little black dress.

"What are you?" the vampire asked, his voice deeper now too. She felt a very slight tingling at the edge of her hearing and knew he was trying one of his vampire tricks on her.

"Someone you can't mesmerize into telling you anything and getting out of the way," she snapped. "Stop wasting your energy. You'll just get more desperate for blood."

"Who are you?" the vampire said, no longer with that edge of power in his voice. He actually sounded truly baffled.

"I told you. A concerned bystander. Now, are we done yet? I'm hungry." She winced a little and to the vampire said, "Sorry. That was thoughtless. But really, you need to feed on someone willing. The wizard is not."

"He owes Gabriel."

"That may well be true. But he's not willing to feed you." She narrowed her eyes at the wizard. "You *did* just promise to feed Gabriel right? What deal did you make?"

"Gabriel and Gabriel only," he said. "I wouldn't willingly feed a lesser vampire."

The vampire snarled and charged again. This time he got tossed up into the air and he crashed against the metal fire escape above them. The black bird who was still sitting on the railing watching the exchange screeched in protest.

Cary frowned up at that bird. The fact that it was still there. And that it didn't fly away when the vampire hit its perch was…weird.

The vampire slamming to the ground at her feet brought her attention back down from the bird. "Why?" she asked him. "You know you're not getting through me."

"But why not?" the vampire hissed, climbing to his feet. "You're human. Not a wizard. A witch?"

"No," she said primly. "Concerned. Citizen. Now stop or you'll get hurt."

"I'm not leaving without my promised food," the vampire said.

"I'm not feeding you," the wizard said.

Cary let out a long, pained breath and shook her head.

They were at a standoff because she wasn't allowing either of them to hurt each other. Or any other innocent bystander. Did this count as a Mexican standoff? She wasn't sure. She'd have to look it up.

Anyway, with neither man backing down, she was stuck here until something broke the stalemate.

This was going to be a long night.

4

*a*s Cary waited for the vampire and wizard to realize this fight was a waste of time, her stomach growled. Loudly. Damn. She would have thought the stench of garbage behind the nightclub would have dampened her appetite but apparently not.

To Deacon, she called, "I don't supposed you'd go get us some pizza. Or sandwiches or something? I'm hungry. And it looks like I'm going to be here for a while, until these idiots decide to call it quits."

"I'm not leaving you here alone," he said, his voice deep and rumbly with his leopard right at the surface.

He was trying so hard not to rush into the middle of things. She really appreciated that.

"Fair enough," she said. "Thanks for staying out of the way."

There was a grunt she couldn't interpret. Which was probably for the best.

The wizard frowned at the shadows. "Why is your shifter boyfriend *not* interfering?" he asked.

"You expect me to tell you things when you won't tell me about the deal you made to get into this mess? No."

The wizard snarled slightly but shrugged. "You want to know the truth? I made the deal because Master vampire blood, when handled right, has healing properties. I needed a cure for…someone, and I was desperate.”

“Someone you love?”

The wizard didn't answer. He glared at the vampire, not meeting her gaze.

“Did the cure work?”

“No.” The answer was clipped, toneless.

“I'm sorry,” she said quietly.

The wizard blinked and glanced at her before looking away. He pressed his lips together and didn't respond.

“Is that why you said you don't owe Gabriel?” she asked, her tone softened by compassion.

“No,” he said again. “I made the deal. And I already fulfilled it. I don't owe him or his vampires anything else.”

“Wait, what?” She frowned between him and the vampire. “You've already given blood to Gabriel?”

“Gabriel claims you still owe him,” the vampire said.

“Gabriel is lying,” the wizard spat. “I gave him his feed. This is bullshit.”

The vampire hesitated a moment. Enough that Cary knew he had his doubts. But instead of leaving and going to find a willing victim, he threw himself at Cary's shield again.

“Gabriel gave you to me,” the vampire said. “I will feed.”

“Well, this is just great,” she said. “We're gonna be here all night if he doesn't go away.”

“Not if you'd just let me kill him,” the wizard said.

Cary watched the vampire throwing himself at her, hunting for a way through her shield. He really did look like shit for a vampire. She wasn't going to put him into the good guy category, not by a long stretch, but something had happened to get him to this stage. And she had a feeling it was something Gabriel had done to him—either a punishment or a test or some other nonsensical vampire thing—and then for reasons known only to Gabriel, he'd sicced the starving minion on the wizard.

The fact that she still didn't know either of their names was irritating.

Anyway, something stunk about the whole situation, more so than the unemptied trash bin a few yards away. But since she'd probably gotten all the information she was going to get from them, she wasn't likely to know the underlying whys. Which was also irritating. Though not unprecedented in her line of work.

She was nosey, though, so it kind of bugged her. Especially since the not-knowing part right now meant she couldn't let the wizard just willy-nilly kill the vampire. She was here to protect the wizard—for reasons known only to her bosses—and not the vampire. Yet because the vampire was starving, and wasn't in his most logical state of mind, letting him be killed didn't seem right either.

A conundrum.

"Can you kill him?" Cary wondered aloud to the wizard. If he could kill a vampire so easily, and that took care of the threat, and he was supposed to be the good guy in all this, why the hell had her bosses sent her here? Why not just let the wizard kill the vampire?

"In the state he's in," the wizard said. "Yes. He can't move fast enough to avoid my bolts forever."

The snarl in the wizard's voice made her give him a look. He ignored the look.

"If you kept throwing bolts at him until he slowed down," she said, "or any other spell for that matter, you'd cause a lot of damage and possibly kill someone else. That seems like a stupid plan."

"I'm not the one who attacked first," the wizard said. "He came after me. I have a right to defend myself."

"Yeah, yeah, but not a right to kill innocent people."

She was starting to think that really was the whole point of her being here. Not so much to protect the wizard or the vampire, but to prevent the fight that could have hurt others. It made a lot more sense. Neither of these guys really needed her help in this. They were fully grown men. Fully grown men should be able to take care of themselves. And if they couldn't, well then whose fault was that but their own.

She admitted to a certain bias when it came to protecting adult men. It was a character flaw. She wasn't particularly proud of it either because sometimes they really did need protecting.

It was just, in this particular case, she wasn't seeing it. The wizard was apparently capable of defending himself and fighting back. The vampire, even weak from hunger—and maybe a little crazed given how relentlessly he kept throwing himself at her shield—was strong enough to defend himself. If they wanted to get into a fight, then that was technically their business. As long as they didn't hurt anyone else.

Still, the situation bothered her. She was here for a reason, which she might never know, and the Nags felt compelled to have her protect the *wizard*. Not innocent bystanders. They were specific about her protecting the *wizard* this time around.

Why?

"I really hate not understanding," she muttered.

"It's easy," the wizard said. "Get out of my way. I'll kill him. This will be over."

She rolled her eyes. "First, I wasn't talking to you. Second, no. Third, there's more going on here than you know, and so I'm not letting anyone kill anyone tonight."

"Gabriel broke the deal. He'll just keep sending his people after me. He has to know I can kill his minions or he won't stop."

"I'm sure he's well aware of what you can do, or he wouldn't have agreed to your bargain in the first place. Aren't you even a little curious why he sent a starving vampire to feed on you? Why a weakened vampire instead of one at full strength? One you stood a chance of killing?"

"I am *not weak*," the vampire roared and threw himself off her shield again. This time he created sparks trying to push through her.

"Stop that," she said. "You catch on fire, I have no way of putting you out right now. And you'll have only yourself to blame."

The vampire backed off, reluctantly, and shook his hands, putting out the flames. His singed skin healed but slower than was typical for a vampire.

She frowned. Something about all this really really stunk—and it wasn't just the gross burnt-meat smell.

For some reason, she glanced up. The black bird was still there. Watching. Its little black eyes unblinking as it took in the scene below.

That was definitely not a normal bird.

"I don't care why he did this," the wizard said, "only that he did."

"Well, that's a very close-minded attitude that isn't going to help you much going forward in life," she said. "I thought wizards sought out knowledge. Hungered for all the information. That kind of thing."

"I just want my brother to live. I don't give two flying fucks about vampires and their games."

Well. Cary closed her eyes briefly. That answered her question. And knowing the wizard was just trying to save his brother made her a lot less annoyed about being here.

"What's wrong with him?" she asked. Then winced. That sounded more gruff and blunt than she'd intended. She cleared her throat. "Sorry. I… He's dying?" No less blunt. She hoped her tone was better that time to help cut the pointed question.

"He's suffering. I want his suffering to stop, but not the way he wants it to."

The wizard's voice, if anything, got harder and angrier as he spoke. He snarled at the vampire and another ball of glowing blue-green light formed in his palm.

If she was reading this guy right, his brother was suicidal and he was working against time to keep his brother from taking that last fatal step. She had no idea what vampire blood had to do with any of this. She'd have to do a little research herself if the wizard wasn't in the mood to spill any more information on accident. But her heart hurt for the poor guy now.

"Okay," she said quietly. To the vampire, she said, "Gabriel is playing a game. With you and with this guy." She pointed over her shoulder to her charge. "If you're not going to explain that game to us, maybe you should just consider it yourself. Why you've been used as a pawn and to what end? What do you get out of this?"

"That's none of your business," the vampire said, snarling at her.

"Yeah, yeah, so you've said. I'm not asking you to tell me

anything." She shrugged. "Although, I'm super curious and I will definitely listen if you *want* to tell me everything. But I'm just asking you to consider all this yourself. I'm not letting you get at the wizard. I'm not letting him kill you to get you guys to back off. And though it pains me to say it, I really can just stand here all night long preventing this fight. So it might behoove all of us for you to consider the whys of all this and decide if it's really in your best interest to keep throwing yourself uselessly against my shields, draining away what little energy you have left. You're going to end up too weak to feed."

She held up a hand when he snarled and tried to launch at her. "You're already moving slower than you were just a few minutes ago. I can *see* you moving."

That should give the bastard a wakeup call. She shouldn't be able to see him moving. Granted, her Protector magic actually did allow her to see vampires and shifters at their top speeds, just blurry. Still, even with that, she could tell this guy was moving a lot slower than he would be capable of at full strength.

The scary part was that even if this guy did manage to find a willing victim, he might just drain them dry, accidentally killing them in his desperation to fill up again.

This was so so not good. What the hell Gabriel?

From the shadows, Deacon said, "I can end this now if you like."

There was a very distinct growl in his voice. The sound of his leopard at the surface and his control on the edge.

She swallowed hard as her heartbeat kicked up a few notches. "Got it. We're good. Don't shift."

They were a long way from his car and his ready supply of backup clothing. He was notoriously bad at taking his clothes off *first* before shifting, which meant he wrecked a lot of his clothing. And since walking through downtown Portland with either a leopard *or* a naked man would draw more attention than either of them wanted, everyone was better off right now if Deacon didn't lose control of his leopard and come charging in.

But the longer this lasted, the harder it would be on him.

And the more likely things would devolve into disaster.

5

*C*ary frowned at the vampire. He'd paused in his attacks on her shield but his gaze darted around, as if he were looking for a way through her.

"You're weak from hunger," she said to him, "but you aren't getting an unwilling wizard meal. What else can we do for you so you aren't so weak, but so you don't kill someone, and so you will go away and leave the wizard here alone? Especially since it has now emerged that he's fulfilled his obligation to your Master."

The vampire scowled. "What?"

"I just outlined everything that's happened up to this point so that we can find a solution. Try to keep up. Or has your weakened state made it difficult for you to follow logic?" She said the last in all seriousness. It was entirely possible—in fact very likely—a starved vampire wouldn't be able to think logically.

Did she have sympathy for a vampire now? No. That didn't seem right. Feeling sympathy for both a wizard—who'd hit her with an energy bolt—and a vampire—who'd happily rip her throat out—seemed like a very silly thing to do.

Figured she was that ridiculous.

She sighed. Well, it was out there. "Can we find a way to feed you on someone willing without you killing them?" she asked the vampire more slowly.

Instead of answer, he threw himself at her again, his snarling mouth opened so wide, his jaw looked unhinged. His face seemed to be growing more elongated and skeletal as the moments wore on. His teeth were long and sharp and very white, but his gums were black and his breath reeked of death and rot.

To be fair, vampire breath always smelled like that. Their mesmerism usually disguised the stench.

"You have any ideas?" she asked the wizard as the vampire clawed at her. Wherever his body maintained sustained contact with her shield, his skin smoked.

He had to be one damned strong vampire under normal circumstances.

The wizard answered her question by throwing another energy bolt at the vampire.

The bolt hit her shield, the energy sizzling around her harmlessly.

"That's not what I meant," she said to the wizard.

But he wasn't listening to her anymore. And neither was the vampire.

Suddenly, there were bolts flying and vampire snarling and screeching to get past her, and between the noise and the stray flickers of energy and the growing sounds of people at the front of the nightclub, Cary's nerves were shot.

She was supposed to be on a date, damn it.

She stomped her foot on the ground in what she considered a pretty epic princess pout, even on a broken high heel, and shouted, "Enough!"

To her utter surprise, both wizard and vampire jolted back from her, hard, as if she'd charged in between them and her shield had thrown them backward. But that shouldn't have happened when she was already standing here.

Weird.

The fighting stopped. They both blinked at her.

She stared back without blinking.

"Are we done yet?" she asked when the silence had finally stretched to breaking point.

"Cary?" Deacon called.

"Fine," she said back, still glaring at the two idiots responsible for her ruined date.

"There are people in front of the building who heard the noise," Deacon called, moving a little out of the shadows so she could see him. His eyes were glowing yellow, very obviously now. His leopard was right there, ready to rip out of him at the slightest nudge.

And innocent people were about to come around the corner because human curiosity was an absolute guarantee of occasional stupidity.

The kind of stupidity she'd committed herself more than once.

"All right," she said to the wizard and vampire, who still hadn't deigned to tell her their names, "we're about to get an audience. That will be bad for all involved. And since I'm not letting you—" she broke off to glare at the wizard, "—*either* of you, kill innocent people, and since this fight seems to be at a stalemate, you two have a choice. You can call it a night, go your separate ways, and maybe start asking sensible questions about why Gabriel set you both up this way. Or you can reveal yourselves to the human population and their plethora of cellphone cameras, enrage most of the magical community, including the vampire Master of the City, and end up hunted into the ground by both humans *and* other magical entities. The choice is yours."

She crossed her arms over her chest, hoping for a defiant stance. She wasn't sure she carried it off in her one good heel while standing on her toes on the foot with the broken heel. A more graceful woman might have. She wobbled and had to spread her legs a little more and brace herself to hold the pose. Which wasn't exactly the coolest of looks.

Ah well.

Both vampire and wizard looked back toward the nightclub. And the sound of humans moving closer.

They'd picked this place to fight, risked human attention from the start. Maybe they didn't care about being revealed. But most of the preternatural world preferred not to show themselves to humans for a whole host of reasons—some even conflicting with others—and she doubted, given their circumstances, either of these numskulls wanted to be the ones to expose their particular group to the outside world.

Before either could make a decision, though, the black bird overhead made a loud screeching noise.

And two new vampires moved out of the shadows at the far side of the nightclub, from the direction opposite the approaching humans.

They were both radiant in their well-fed health. Pale skin almost glowing in the bad, back-alley lighting. Eyes sparkling blue and brown respectively. The woman had blond hair that hung to her hips and heart-shaped lips painted perfectly red. She wore a little black dress and heels, too, but she carried the look off a lot better than Cary did. The man wore a suit and tie, but the kind of fitted, slightly short at the ankle suit that bespoke modern hipster rather than conservative business man. He also had long blond hair, though his only came to his shoulders, and he'd topped his breathtakingly handsome head with a bowler hat skewed slightly to the side. That shouldn't have looked quite so good, but he made it work.

These two were what Cary expected vampires to look like when out and about—glamorous, beautiful, awe-inducing. They were obviously *not* suffering from malnutrition.

The first vampire snarled at the newcomers. "No! He said I could feed on the wizard."

"Time to leave, Roger," the female vampire said.

Roger? What kind of name was Roger for a vampire?

"You're done for now," the male vampire said. To Cary, he added, "We'll ensure he feeds properly. He won't be a problem."

"That would be good," she said, frowning at them.

The woman smiled seductively at Deacon as he moved farther into view. "Hello, handsome."

Cary's frown turned into a scowl. But Deacon growled at the greeting, and the glow in his eyes intensified, so she had a feeling he wasn't pleased by the vampire's comehither smile. That was good. Maybe. Unless this led to someone attacking someone else. Again.

She moved just a little so she stood in front of both Deacon and the wizard. Having the wizard at her back where she couldn't see him well was a little nerve-racking, though.

The male vampire ignored the exchange and tilted his head slightly to look around Cary at the wizard. "You will not be approached by a vampire again. You have paid your service."

"Then why attack this time?" the wizard said, his voice deep and harsh.

The vampire didn't answer. He faced Cary and said, "We're finished here."

He gave her a slight nod, glanced up at the black bird, and then all three vampires were gone.

ary blinked a few times. In the moment after the vampires' departure, her brain registered the swift movements of their exit, the blur of motion that had been them. They'd grabbed the first vampire on their way out and the slight echo of his protest remained. But all of that took longer for her brain to process than it had taken to happen. And she only caught up to it all after they were gone.

Vampires were scary.

She looked up. The bird cawed once, flapped its wings, and flew off into the darkness over the city. Cary narrowed her eyes.

"That felt a bit like a test," she said quietly to Deacon.

"Possible," he said. His voice was still gravely and rough and deep from his leopard being so near the surface.

The sound made her shiver but not from fear. Which was weird and probably not good. She blamed the mate thing.

"Why?" she asked, mostly to herself.

And who? Gabriel? That wouldn't be good. But…if he'd set this up, were the Nags in on the test—she *was* officially in a test year—or were they as much pawns to the vampire games as she?

Or was she just seeing conspiracies where there were none?

She faced the wizard just as a couple of hapless humans poked their heads around the building. Deacon moved closer to her, wrapping an arm around her shoulders. The wizard wasn't showing off his energy bolts anymore. And except for the deep yellow glow in Deacon's eyes, they probably just looked like normal people standing around talking.

At least, she hoped that's what they looked like.

The humans who'd come to investigate looked a little confused. They glanced around, shrugged, and head back to the front of the building, to the lights and crowds that would keep them safe from the monsters that bumped around in the shadows.

"You okay?" Cary asked the wizard when they no longer had an audience.

"No. But I wasn't before the vampire attacked."

"Anything we can do?" she asked because, despite everything, he looked very young and tired and sad just then, and her heart went out to him even though she knew she shouldn't feel sorry for him after he'd thrown wizard bolts at her. Technically, he'd been aiming for the vampire so she supposed she could forgive him.

Her skin tingled now that she wasn't protecting anyone anymore, though, and she leaned into Deacon, trying to ease the sensation of ants crawling over her nerves. The tingles weren't as bad as usual for some reason, so that was something. Especially since her twisted ankle was now starting to hurt. And so were her calf muscles after holding herself up on one high heel for so long. Letting Deacon take her weight so she could ease the strain on her muscles seemed entirely too natural.

But she'd worry about that feeling later.

"No," the wizard answered her question. "Nothing anyone can do."

"I'm sorry."

The wizard rubbed a hand over his face. "It is what it is." He sighed. "I suppose I should thank you. If I'd killed him, the vampires wouldn't let me live."

"Probably ought to avoid the vampires for a while," she said. "I don't know what this was all about, but maybe you and your brother take a vacation somewhere. Maybe someplace nice and sunny. The tropics are pleasant this time of year. Little extra light, might even help."

Since she wasn't sure what was wrong with his brother to make him suicidal, she wasn't sure if she'd just given the worst advice ever, or even been unintentionally cruel, but it was too late to take it back. And, with the information the wizard had given her, it was the best she could do.

Actually, avoiding the vampires was always good advice, no matter the circumstances. So there was that.

There was an awkward pause as they all stared at each other. Then the wizard said, "Sorry I hit you with a few energy bolts."

"You're forgiven this time. Don't do it again."

"Yes," Deacon growled. "Don't do that again."

The wizard gave Deacon a wary look before turning back to Cary. "Think I might take your advice. Andy and I haven't been on a vacation in years." He waved vaguely at them and strode off around the side of the building, back toward the front of the nightclub.

Cary and Deacon remained where they were for a long moment.

"You know," Cary said, her head tilted toward Deacon's shoulder. "I now know his brother's name, but not his."

"You know the vampire's name."

"Roger. What the hell kind of vampire is named Roger?"

"I've met one named Tim before."

"That's a terrible name for a vampire, too." They started back around to the front of the nightclub, having given the wizard time to lose himself in the growing night crowds. "I kind of half thought they changed their names when they became undead. You know, took on a new spookier, more elaborate name. To go with the new look."

"So Roger should have become…what?"

"I don't know. Robespierre?"

"Robespierre?"

"I don't know." She huffed. "What do I know about vampire names? Don't laugh."

"Wouldn't think of it."

"Right."

They moved through the crowd outside the nightclub, angling back toward the parking garage.

Cary limped a few yards on her broken heel before finally giving in to the inevitable. "We're going home now, aren't we?"

"I thought pizza, maybe a movie on TV?"

She sighed. And smiled. "That sounds really nice."

She leaned down and pulled off her broken heal, balancing on Deacon's arm. Then she switched feet and removed the intact heel. Her feet were going to be filthy by the time they got back to her place, which meant a shower. Which, if Deacon joined her, meant a nice way to bide their time until the pizza arrived.

She shivered a little and her stomach tightened in anticipation.

Deacon leaned close. "Whatever you're thinking about right now, I approve."

"If I told you I was thinking about pizza?"

He chuckled and the heat of his breath on her cheek made her shiver again. "I wouldn't be even a little surprised," he said. "But that wasn't the only thing you were thinking about." He tapped his nose.

She wanted to scold him for reading her mind again, but she didn't have the energy. Instead, she said, "I was just thinking I'd need a shower after all this. And, you know, I'd hate to bath alone."

His arm tightened around her waist. "Will you let me carry you?" He nodded to her bare feet.

The thought of Deacon carrying her was very tempting. In fact, she was just about to jump up into his arms.

And then that dreaded feeling swept down her spine. Someone needed her help.

The sensation was urgent. She looked around, spotted the man staring at a woman who was happily walking toward the nightclub not paying much attention to the little purse hanging from her shoulder by a very skinny chain.

Cary didn't pause to explain to Deacon. She dropped her shoes and raced forward in the same instant as the man started running.

She got between him and the woman an instant before he reached her. In fact, he was so intent on the woman's purse, he didn't check his lunge for the bag and ended up grabbing Cary's arm instead.

To both their surprise, a sizzle of visible blue electrical energy jolted into him from her arm. He yelped and jumped backward, holding his hand.

"You shocked me," he accused.

"Don't try to steal purses and you won't get hurt," she said, putting her hands on her hips.

The woman behind her had paused. "What the hell?" she said, clutching at her purse.

The man looked at them both, his skin pale under the lamplight. He glanced around, then took off running in the opposite direction, disappearing around the corner.

Cary shook her head. "You okay?" she said to the woman.

"Yeah. Thanks for stopping him. I hate purse snatchers." The woman waved to Cary and spun back toward the nightclub, laughing with her friends as if nothing had just happened, her purse once again dangling unnoticed from her shoulder.

Cary sighed and leaned into Deacon. She didn't bother to question how he'd gotten to her side so fast. She just hoped none of the humans around them noticed.

"She's gonna lose that purse eventually, isn't she?"

"Probably tonight," he agreed. "But at least not to a thief. You okay?"

"The shock he got from grabbing me was weird," she said. "But yeah, otherwise, just fine." Her feet would protest running along the sidewalk barefoot soon, but at least she hadn't stepped in anything gross.

At a glance, she noticed Deacon had her shoes and her purse in one hand. The fact that he'd thought to collect her shoes and hadn't dropped her purse in all the night's chaos made her smile.

She looked up at him. "I'm ready to go home, though. Another bust of a date, huh?"

"We can still salvage the night," he said, his voice dropping into a low, seductive murmur. "I seem to recall something about a bath. And pizza."

The man knew her surprisingly well after only a couple of months. She squeaked in surprise when he swept her up into his arms, but she didn't protest. She was getting used to Deacon carrying her, though she'd never admit to him just how much she enjoyed it.

He probably picked up the scent of her pleasure anyway.

As they headed back to the parking lot—this time with no more Protector detours—she decided pizza and a bath with Deacon was a very very good way to spend the rest of this strange night.

There were a lot worse ways to end a failed date.

THIRD DATE'S THE CHARM

Third times the charm. Right?

For Cary Redmond, Portland's resident magical Protector, going on a simple date with her leopard shifter mate is proving almost impossible. Really, she just wants to get through dinner. After two failed attempts, Cary and Deacon are determined to make this date work.

They even make it all the way to the starter course.

But bad guys show no respect for a Protector's romantic life. And Cary can't ignore her job when there's danger. Because if she does, people die.

1

ary hurried into the restaurant, smoothing her hair. She subtly sniffed the ends of her ponytail. She was pretty sure she'd gotten the smell out. But there were still a few flecks of glitter. That stuff was impossible to wash out.

Deacon stood when he saw her, his smile a welcome and a question in one. And everything about it made her toes curl.

Damn but he was gorgeous. He took her breath away. Golden eyes, dark dark hair which she knew for a fact was thick and silky against her fingers. He'd dressed in black dress slacks and a white button up shirt that showed off his tan skin tone and the magnificent breadth of his shoulders. He had the sleeves rolled up a little, which wasn't as formal as the restaurant seemed to call for, but since it let her admire his forearms, she wasn't about to argue.

He was stunning. Sometimes she could almost forget, almost over-look the sheer Greek god-like perfection of him. And then he'd smile and she'd melt. And her awareness of him would roar back to life.

They were trying for a proper date. Again. Hoping third time would be the charm. The first time, they hadn't gotten through the opening credits of their movie before her job had interrupted. The second, they never even made it to the theater.

This time, they'd agreed to start with dinner.

He'd picked a nice restaurant too, with real table clothes, dim mood lighting, quiet classical music playing in the background, and an elegantly dressed hostess. The place smelled like rich sauces and good wine.

But she'd been given a last minute job that afternoon, so of course, she was late.

A quick rescue her bosses had said. Nothing that would stop the date, according to her nicer boss, Wisat. So she and Deacon had agreed to meet at the restaurant—he'd argued to go with her on the job, but she'd persuaded him to sit this one out. He'd gotten sucked into a lot of her work since they met. Really, that wasn't fair for him.

"Everything okay?" he asked against her ear.

She shivered a little at the heat, then grinned when he held her chair for her as she sat. "Ah, that's very gentlemanly of you."

He chuckled. "My mother would have my head if I didn't occasionally mind my manners."

"Ha!"

She settled her coat on the back of the seat as he returned to his. She'd decided to try a dress and heels one last time, but she'd chosen low heels and a more casual black wrap dress for this date. She glanced around. Maybe a little too casual for the fancy restaurant. But she hadn't had time to fret over her clothing choices tonight.

The one thing the last minute assignment had done for her was distract her so she couldn't get all worried and anxious about this date. She'd been almost too nervous for conversation the first time they'd tried this. Despite the fact they were already sleeping together and spent all their time together to accommodate the mate bond thing and his dodgy control. The second attempted date had only been slightly better, but she'd still been edgy and irrationally nervous.

Those times, the date had felt significant, important to get right. And she'd been a wreck.

This time, well she still felt like it was important that this went well, and there was still a little giddy, edginess under the surface.

Okay, maybe more than a little. But they'd failed at this date business twice already. Things really couldn't get worse this time.

And she'd been so busy doing her job, she hadn't had time to work herself up into a lather. Which was nice because she wanted to enjoy the food at this fancy restaurant, seeing as how he'd gone to all the trouble of bringing her here. Plus, she was starving.

Then she looked across the table at him, at his slight smile and that glitter in his dark golden eyes, and her pulse started pumping harder. His smile widened as if he could hear her heartbeat, which given he was a leopard shifter with superb hearing, he probably could.

She pulled in a slow breath, trying to settle the wash of giddiness. Really, this was getting ridiculous. A date shouldn't be a big deal. Especially since this was their *third* attempt! And they ate dinner together all the time. Nothing new there. She'd worried about having things to discuss with him on a date, but they always found stuff to talk about. And when they didn't talk, the silences weren't nearly as awkward as she'd have assumed given they were still getting to know each other.

Given everything, she should be as comfortable with him in this moment as she was with…well, maybe not her best friends, but at least she should be comfortable.

Yet, when she held his gaze in this beautiful setting, his yummy scent reaching out to her across the table, subtle and seductive despite the more overwhelming food smells, she felt turned inside out and upside down. Overwhelmed. Nervous. And a little too warm.

She broke eye contact first because she was afraid she'd start to hyperventilate. His slight, mildly smug smile, which she only caught from the corner of her eye, made her wince.

They waited for the hostess to hand out menus and wish them a good meal before speaking more.

"So no problems with the job?" he asked.

"Nope." She opened her menu, raising her brows a little at the prices. He was showing off. That was kind of sweet.

"You have glitter in your hair," he said.

She made a face. "Fine. The bad guy in this case was a pixie. And this pixie tossed incredibly smelly glitter dust all over the place while he was having a pout because I wouldn't let him switch out a baby in a stroller for a changeling. Which, I might add, was obviously *not* a baby that anyone might confuse and just wander off with. The woman would have noticed her baby was gone and had a fit. The changeling was this little ugly old Fae. Not even a baby or child or anything. A literal grumbling old man with no teeth."

Fae didn't technically age. They were immortal, though they could be killed. But they came in a wide variety of shapes, sizes, and looks, depending on their species. This one had been a brownie and he carried the "little old man" look well. To be fair to the brownie, he'd been just as annoyed at being offered up as a changeling as the baby's mother had been that a stinky pixie tried to kidnap her baby.

Deacon raised his brows. "What was the point of all that, then?"

She raised her hands, palms up. "Got me. Maybe the pixie was in charge of looking after the brownie and got tired of it? Hell if I know. He didn't feel the need to do the bad guy monologue, much to my disappointment."

Amazingly enough, bad guys did tend toward that whole monologuing thing if you got them mad enough. And Cary was really really good at pissing off bad guys so that they talked too much. It was kind of her superpower. Well, that and her *actual* magical Protector powers.

As a Protector—a job she even got paid for—she channeled magic given to her from her bosses, purely defensive powers. She just had to get between a bad guy and a good guy, her shields went up, and she could keep the good guys safe from all sorts of mayhem. Including pouting pixies throwing smelly glitter dust.

Unfortunately, sometimes, especially when magic was involved or when she was throwing herself between bad guys and good guys at the very last second, small, non-deadly things got through her shield. Occasionally, this resulted in weird injuries—her medical records were a mess. In this case, the only thing that got through was a little of the dust.

She brushed at her hair again. "I literally shampooed my hair three times to get this stuff out. Can you still smell it?"

Deacon didn't just have excellent shifter hearing, he also had super shifter smelling. She'd been more worried about his ability to smell the stink than she'd been about the glitter.

"Only very faintly," he said. "Although, I can't imagine how badly that must have smelled at full strength."

"Very very bad," she said. "It's not going to ruin your dinner?"

He smiled and for a full thirty seconds she forgot anything else existed. Wow, the man had a powerful grin. She blinked a few times to refocus on the present.

"Very few things can ruin food for me," he said. "And you'd be surprised at the…range of smells I deal with regularly."

"For once, I'm glad I don't have your super senses." Usually, she envied his ability to scent things like…oh, someone's mood or the fact that they were supposed to be mates. She was still hesitant about the whole thing. Because she wasn't a shifter, because she couldn't *scent* the bond between them the way he could, she was left wondering if it was real.

Not that she was prepared to give him back just yet. She'd gotten used to having him around. But the full, long term implications of it all still overwhelmed her.

Especially since they couldn't seem to just go on a normal date.

"Hopefully, that's the worst that happens tonight," she said, picking up her menu again. "And we can enjoy dinner without interruptions."

He raised his brows, an expression she couldn't decipher, so she decided to let it go. She probably didn't want to know anyway.

"Tell me what you did while I was out rescuing babies from mean, smelly pixies," she said, hoping to move things into proper date conversation territory, pleased she could manage small talk when she kept getting distracted by the way his forearm muscles flexed as he read his menu.

"I made a few work calls," he said.

"Caitlin doing well?"

His younger sister had pretty much taken over running the family business—rescue shelters for all sorts of animals, but their specialty was exotics—because Deacon still wasn't fully in control of his leopard side if he wasn't around Cary. It had to do with the mate bond thing, which he assured her was normal. Leopard's lost a lot of their control after meeting their mates and it took time to settle down. In the meantime, he was too dangerous to be around humans and animals that might challenge his leopard.

Cary still wasn't sure how she felt about having that responsibility. Neither of them could help his control issues, except to ensure he stayed with her as often as possible. But knowing her presence was required or else he'd become extremely dangerous was a pretty over-whelming bit of knowledge.

"She's fine," he said. "Says hi." He glanced up over his menu. "You two are getting along entirely too well"

Cary grinned at that, still looking in her food choices. She'd only met Caitlin for coffee once so far, at Caitlin's insistence, but they'd had a great visit. And their getting to know each other made Deacon edgy, which was such a relief—she wasn't the only one nervous about all this; yay!—she wasn't above needling him about it.

"I like your sister. She's full of good stories." All about Deacon. Mostly embarrassing ones.

He grunted. Her grin widened.

"What are you going to order?" he asked.

A good distraction. Everything looked tasty. And expensive. But tasty.

She ended up picking a steak meal she'd never normally order for herself or even know how to make at home—her cooking skills were limited by…well, disinterest in cooking. They even decided on appe-tizers, a plate of what she assumed were very fancy potato skins since they cost a fortune and had truffle oil on them. Other than the truffle oil, though, the description sounded like regular old potato skins. She liked those, and Deacon was paying, so she didn't complain.

The waiter took their order, very professional and deferential to Deacon, which had her narrowing her eyes at her mate. He even referred to Deacon by name. "Thank you, Mr. Jones. We'll have your appetizers out to you soon."

"Come here a lot?" she asked after the waiter left.

"We occasionally bring some of our big donors here," he said with a shrug. "As a thank you for contributing."

It was, apparently, a big part of his job to schmooze wealthy donors and get people to give money to the shelters. Also, according to both Deacon and his sister, Caitlin was a lot better at that effort than he was.

Her stomach growled as the appetizers appeared.

Deacon grinned. "Hungry?"

"I guess fending off pixie glitter will do that to a woman," she said. The fancy potato skins looked delicious. She couldn't wait for her steak.

She'd just taken her first, glorious, melty cheesy, potato, and truffley bite, when a familiar sensation tingled down her spine. She straightened. Oh no.

Not now.

2

$\mathcal{W}$ho the hell was causing trouble now?

Cary scanned the restaurant, hoping this was a simple, easy to handle issue—someone about to throw a glass of wine on their date, that sort of thing. Hoping in vain because her Protector senses wouldn't have perked up at something so harmless.

When she didn't see anything, she stood. "Sorry," she said to Deacon without looking at him. And headed toward the back of the restaurant, her instincts driving her to the kitchen.

She paused at the swinging silver door, peeked through the rounded window into the kitchen, spotted the small man with a large gun, and rushed inside.

Since the gun was pointing toward a cluster of people, she put herself between the cluster and the gun. And because she did something that most people didn't do—namely move in *front* of a gun instead of trying to run away from it—the gunman took several long moments to blink at her.

When he finally realized he had one more, unexpected, hostage, he snarled. "Who the hell are you?"

"Oh, just a happy customer," she said. "And you would be?"

"The guy with the gun," he said.

85

"Yeah. Noticed. Why?"

"He thought he could fire me. Me! I made this place. He's taking credit for *my* food."

Okay. So disgruntled employee. She assumed one of the people in the cluster must be the head chef.

"You're little better than a dishwater, Philip," a man said over Cary's shoulder. "Don't you dare try to take credit for my creations."

Oh boy. "Uhm," she said, turning slightly to address the chef. "Better not to aggravate the guy with the gun until *after* he no longer has a gun. Okay?"

"I don't know who you are, lady," the disgruntled employee said, "but you got a death wish, I'm happy to oblige."

"Wait," she said as he lifted the gun and fingered the trigger. He actually paused, which kind of surprised her. "Huh. I didn't expect you to actually wait." She shook her head. "Anyway…"

"Shut up."

"So much for waiting."

"You stepped in where you don't belong. I'm not to blame for your death. You are."

She sighed. She really really hated it when the bad guys didn't take responsibility for their actions. "I'm not the one pulling any triggers," she said, annoyed now. "You're the one with the gun, holding people hostage, looking to kill. Don't blame other people for your problems, you asshole. All this and everything that follows is on you."

She didn't see Deacon at the door, but she caught movement from the corner of her eye. And she was sure he was there somewhere. When she had to protect someone, and he happened to be around, he got involved. He just couldn't seem to help himself.

Since she couldn't actually do anything about the gunman except stand here and keep him from killing anyone, she did her part. She stood there, arms crossed. And when the sharp retort of the gun sounded, she continued to stand there as the people behind her screamed.

She hated guns.

The hail of bullets made her frown. There were an awful lot of them for a single gun. She spread her hands out, an unconscious move to keep the six people she was protecting safely together.

When she sensed someone behind her move, she glanced back and shouted over the noisy gunfire, "Don't! Just stay there. You're fine. But not if you try to run."

The woman she'd snapped at blinked at her. Her eyes were wide, the pupils dilated, and there was an awful lot of white showing around her brown irises.

Cary took pity. "Listen, you notice how you're okay right now, right?" It was way too noisy for the woman to hear her, though, so she gestured at their surroundings and the woman's uninjured body.

The woman blinked again and looked around. No one had been shot. The wall behind them, the hanging pots, some of the dishes, all took the brunt of the gunfire. Things broke and shattered. A plate all ready to go out took a bullet and sent porcelain and little toast chunks flying. But none of it got through her protections.

Cary hated guns because she usually couldn't get between them and the good guys in time to avoid some weird injury. Bullets just moved too fast. They wouldn't penetrate her skin, and only the first one usually caused any issue, but still, they were a literal pain. If she got between the gun and the potential victims in time, however, nothing got through and that was a lot more pleasant.

The ear-splitting rattatat of gunfire finally died.

Cary took a minute to look at her charges. Everyone looked in shock. But no blood. Yay, Protector shields!

She faced the bad guy again and shook her head. "You really are an asshole. And you deserve what you get."

Deacon moved, so fast he was a blur. One moment there was a man holding a gun, looking stupefied that he hadn't been able to kill anyone. The next, Deacon was holding the gun and the man was face down on the ground, screaming about his broken arm.

"You definitely deserve broken bones," Cary said. "And a lot worse." She smiled at Deacon. "Thanks. And thanks for not rushing in before the bullets stopped flying. That would have pissed me off."

"I've learned that about you." He snarled down at the man under him. The man screamed again and tried to crawl away. Deacon stepped on his lower back to keep him in place. "You're lucky I didn't rip your arm off," he murmured.

The menace in his voice made her shiver. And not in fear, which didn't reflect well on her character.

Outside the closed kitchen door, she could now hear all the screaming and panic. Shit. The police would be here soon. That was good for all the human civilians but not so good for her and Deacon.

She glanced down at the small semi-circle of flattened bullets in front of her. There would be more bullets that hit their mark around the kitchen, destroying the room. But this semi-circle in front of the staff, and the lack of any injuries, was a pretty revealing piece of evidence she'd rather the cops didn't see.

The problem with her job was it was impossible to explain to ordinary law enforcement without risking a forced trip to a mental hospital. The good thing about her job was that everything usually happened so fast, the witnesses told weirdly believable stories the cops would buy— or the stories were so wildly divergent, the cops gave up trying to make real sense of what had happened.

It helped that she was a relatively average looking person. Not too tall or too short. Age hard to determine. Hair that could be dark blond, light brown, or some variation of those shades. Usually dressed in non-descript clothes. And a pleasantly ordinary face that people had trouble remembering clearly.

She consoled herself with the idea that they couldn't remember her face because they were too busy being terrified by what had just happened and never really got a good look at her. It was easier on her ego than thinking she was *that* ordinary looking.

She made eye contact with Deacon as she tried to subtly drag her foot through the neat line of spent bullets, then nodded to the front of the restaurant and all the noise. He nodded back. They needed to leave this to the authorities and try not to get dragged into it all.

"Everyone is okay, right?" she said over her shoulder. When that was confirmed by a series of nods and grunts and mumbles, she said,

"Someone should probably check on the people in the main room. Sounds like things are getting chaotic out there."

The head chef immediate started barking orders at his staff, in a tone that made Cary's shoulders tense. Maybe it was good she and Deacon wouldn't be able to show their faces here again. The chef sounded like an ass even if he made good food.

She started toward Deacon so they could make their way out the back door, when she noticed movement at his feet. The gunman was squirming a little again, but there was a strangeness to the movement that caught her attention. She looked closer. Frowned. Blinked. Stared.

Realized…

Oh shit.

"Deacon, move!"

3

Growing up, Cary hadn't considered herself the soldier type. She'd been the kid giving tea parties to her pets, trying to mediate conflicts between her dog and the cats, and running around her backyard pretending to ride a unicorn while exploring a dragon's den. She wasn't the soldier-fighting-wars-and-throwing-herself-on-bombs-to-save-her-fellow-soldiers type of girl.

And she'd always just assumed that was her actual personality type.

Right up to the minute she threw herself onto a person strapped to a bomb just as the bomb went off.

The impact robbed her of breath, hurt like all hell, and made her see stars. Or maybe that was the light from the explosion? She couldn't really tell. The sound made her ears ring so badly she couldn't hear.

Weirdly, she did notice the drip of blood from her nose rolling warmly down her lip. She lifted onto her hands and knees, then touched the blood. Ugh, that was going to freak Deacon out. He wasn't good with her bleeding.

When the spots in her eyes cleared enough for her to see, she glanced down.

She really shouldn't have.

Her shields had allowed her to keep the blast contained and save everyone in the restaurant. Yay magical Protector shields to the rescue again! Unfortunately, the bomb had still gone off. She hadn't reached the bomber in time to save his life. Frankly, she wasn't even sure she'd have been able to. Her powers were weird and sometimes reacted in amazing and unpredictable ways. But mostly, they were just a shield between disaster and innocent people, not there to keep a bad person from doing a bad thing.

And, boy, had this guy done a bad thing.

Sometimes, her powers even reflected someone's attack back on them. Mostly, that happened with magic attacks, when a spell would rebound off her shields and ended up killing the caster of the spell. In this case, her magic had contained the blast but the shock of all that released energy had pulverized the man who'd triggered it. It was hard to tell the mess under her had even been human at one stage.

So gross.

She felt bile rising in her throat and was terrified she'd throw up and add more mess to the already gruesome scene. She tried to push away but her limbs shook and trembled too much for her to stand. Her ribs hurt—at least a few were probably cracked—and the ringing in her ears hadn't stopped yet. After that single drip of blood, her nose wasn't bleeding anymore. That was nice. She might have a cut on her fore-head, but she didn't seem to have the energy anymore to reach up and see. It was all she could do just to stay crouched *above* the mess beneath her. She really really *really* didn't want to fall back into all that...

Ugh, she couldn't.

Trying hard not to breathe deeply or through her nose, and grateful in that moment she didn't have Deacon's sense of smell, she rocked back until she could sit up onto her knees. She glance down at her dress and winced. The black color hid most of the blood and...stuff, but the cotton material was shiny and sticky with the bomber's remains.

She swallowed a gag. There went another dress. But at least the skirt was long enough she wasn't kneeling in anything with her bare legs. And she hadn't broken a heel this time. Bonus.

Some of the chaos around her finally started to sink in. The noise was still muffled and her brain was moving too slowly to really respond yet. But, yeah, this was gonna require a lot of clean up and explanation.

Deacon's hands on her shoulders were like a warm comforting blanket, so she leaned back into him.

She could sort of hear his voice but had to focus on his mouth and read his lips to figure out what he was saying.

"Why are you still alive?"

She snorted and waved a hand vaguely in front of her face. "You know. Just a talent I have."

He let out a visible breath and shook his head. She couldn't read his expression at all. Couldn't tell what his mood was. He looked surprisingly neutral. Since she'd been expecting more of a reaction, that was a little disconcerting.

"We need to leave very fast," she said, hoping he could hear her over the chaos around them. Especially since she wasn't entirely sure if she was speaking aloud or not. She couldn't tell. She knew she was moving her mouth, but air moving over her vocal chords…? That was a tossup.

She tried to push to her feet, but everything was wobbly and trembling and off balance. She was gonna be ticked off if she'd damaged her inner ear bones. Oh, they'd heal like everything else, but it was just one more irritating injury to be annoyed by. Her ribs hurt like a bitch, too. Standing didn't seem entirely possible in that moment. But even in her still dazed state, she was aware of the movement around her, the chaos, and the inevitability of the police showing up at any minute.

She really didn't have a good answer for why she wasn't dead.

"I may need to swing by the hospital, too," she said to Deacon. "One a little far away from all this." She pointed to her side. "Cracked ribs, I think."

He let out another visible breath. Then very gently, picked her up, arm under knees and the other behind her back, cradling her easily. His physical strength was a marvel. She might even be getting to enjoy having him carry her around like this. Although, she wasn't going to admit that out loud.

"Can you deal with my speed?" he said close to her ear.

She could just hear him over the restaurant noise and the ringing in her ears. "I will if it gets us out of here quickly."

"Hold on."

She closed her eyes because experience had taught her moving at shapeshifter speeds was both exhilarating and left her faintly nauseated if she watched the world blur around her. She wasn't sure she could take the nausea on top of all her other aches and pains.

When he stopped moving, she opened her eyes. They were on a quiet, dark street on the opposite side of the downtown area.

"Wow," she said. "Thank you for getting us so far away so quickly. Sorry about ruining another location for you, though."

Neither of them should probably show their faces at that restaurant again. If it survived after all the mess.

She winced when she remembered, "They know you. Is that going to cause issues with the authorities? When someone realizes neither of us died?"

Deacon shrugged. "I'll take care of it if there are questions." At her skeptical look, his icy expression finally cracked a little. "You keep forgetting, I have had call to deflect the attention of the police myself once or twice. Plus, I'm rich. It's easier to do with money."

She snorted at that, but the laugh made her ribs hurt. "Ouch."

"Fuck," he muttered.

For the first time, she heard his anger. "Worried you, did I? Sorry."

"How the hell did you survive?"

She shrugged. "It's what I do. Although, I have to admit, that was the first time I've been blown up. At least, you know, by conventional methods."

"Conventional methods?"

"Non-magical stuff. Obviously, I've had magical bombs detonate around me before."

"Obviously," he said, his hands tightening on her in a quick, reflexive hug. "Your job is the most terrifying thing I've ever had to deal with."

She cupped his cheek in her palm. "Scared me when I thought I wouldn't get there in time. You were standing right there."

She swallowed hard, for the first time allowing herself to feel and consider what could have been. The pain of it made her body hurt more than her cracked ribs and still ringing ears. The what-might-have-beens were going to give her nightmares.

She could read his expression now, that combination of anger and terror. Those emotions churned in her gut, and she could see them in the tightness of his jaw, the lines around is eyes and mouth, the deep furrows on his brow. His heartbeat was racing against her side and she was positive it wasn't from the run across the city.

"Guess we didn't do so well on our third attempt at a date either," she said. "Although, me with broken ribs and you carrying me away from the scene... Kind of reminiscent of the night we met, isn't it?"

"That doesn't help." He let out a long sigh, and the tightness in his jaw relaxed. "You'd think I'd be used to this by now. Or at least, I'd expect these regular heart attacks from fear. Given that first night."

"Ha! That night was yours and Jaxer's fault. Don't blame me."

Her faery mentor and Deacon had hatched a plan to catch an evil teenage wizard up to no good, and Deacon had needed rescuing. Jaxer had sent Cary in to save the day. The rest was history.

"I don't ever blame you," Deacon said. "I blame all the evil people in the world. If not for them, you wouldn't have to do this all the time."

"True. But then I'd need to go job hunting. And my resume is a little thin now."

He shook his head, not really amused by her joke. She couldn't blame him. It hadn't been much of one anyway.

"We're not far from a hospital," he said. "I can carry you there."

"I parked in one of the garages. That's gonna cost a fortune, leaving the car there overnight." She sighed. Good thing she got paid for this job of hers.

"I'll take care of it," he said as he started up the street.

"You don't have to, but that's sweet to offer."

She studied her surroundings, placing the hospital he was heading toward. She hadn't been there in a while. That was good. Maybe the doctors wouldn't give her the *look* this time. Her medical records were so full of weird injuries, a lot of the ER doctors worried about her. She couldn't blame them. And it was nice to know they cared. But she wasn't in the mood to explain that she wasn't being abused.

"We really suck at dates," she said. "Don't we?"

He shrugged. "Depends on your perspective. You've saved a lot of lives on our last three attempts."

She made a face. There was that. "You don't suppose all our dates will go this way, do you?"

"It's sort of turning into a tradition now. We try a date. You save some people. We spend the rest of the evening doing the cleanup." He gave her a sideways look. "For the sake of my heart, I could do without the needed hospital trip, but otherwise…"

She rolled her eyes because they were the only thing on her body that didn't ache. "I'm not sure we should consider this a good tradition."

"We'll get an uninterrupted date one of these days," he said. Although, he didn't sound all that convinced of his own statement.

She leaned into him, taking comfort in his scent, his strength, his warmth on the cold night—she had no idea how she was going to get her coat back but at least it hadn't been her Marianne-made leather jacket with all the magic pockets. And she'd finally given up the idea of a date-night purse and put her keys and wallet into the pockets in her dress, so that was one less thing to worry about.

She noticed, too late, that the blood on her dress had smeared across his dress shirt, though. There was no way to hide the red stains on white material. Damn. How were they going to explain that? She wondered if they could convince a medical doctor it was ketchup and not blood.

If they did, she wasn't sure she'd be able to trust the doctor with her cracked ribs.

She decided they'd worry about explanations when they got to the ER.

"Sorry about your shirt," she said, gesturing at the red stain soaking through. She couldn't seem to smell the blood and…stuff anymore. Which was a mercy. She wondered—though not enough to ask—if the stink bothered him. If it did, he showed no signs, likely for her sake. But if it really didn't, she wasn't sure she wanted to know why blood and guts smells didn't bother him.

"I've got more shirts," he murmured.

"You looked good in this one."

"I'm glad you approve."

She smiled a little. "You know," she said. "I will just be happy if we can get through dinner one of these days. If we manage that, I'll call it a successful date."

"Fair enough. I like a woman with low expectations."

She chuckled. Then winced. "Don't make me laugh. It hurts."

"Sorry." He kissed her forehead.

"So. We'll try again?" she asked.

"We'll try again." He met her gaze. "And again. Until we get it right. Or at least until you get fed."

She grinned. "Sounds like a good plan."

They were silent for a while, and Cary let the quiet night and Deacon's heat soothe her jangled nerves.

"I did have something I wanted to discuss tonight," he said into the quiet as he turned a corner heading toward the small hospital.

She raised her brows at him.

"My mother has invited us to visit. She'd like us to travel down next week. She's eager to meet you." He paused, sighed quietly. "Actually, she's pretty insistent now."

Cary blinked at the emergency room doors as they slid open. Deacon's mother was insisting on meeting her?

Oh boy.

DINNER WITH THE JONESES

A family dinner with leopard shifters…what could go wrong?

Cary Redmond's first introduction to her leopard shifter boyfriend's family proved a little more interesting and fraught than she might have liked. Okay, the trip was a disaster. So Deacon's mother declares a do-over. And no one argues with the Jones family matriarch. They even agree to come up to Portland, into Cary's territory, for the big meal.

What could possibly go wrong?

Unfortunately, in Cary's world, anything that can, usually does. And when her bosses show up with a job, she can't refuse. Magical Protectors don't get time off for family events…

Not when there are innocent people to protect and monsters on the loose.

~

Author's Note: This story takes place about a week after the events of The Trouble with Leopard Queens and Shifter Wars (Cary Redmond Book 3) and contains spoilers for the novel.

~

1

----

ary stared up at the apartment building, her lips pursed. It was a nice building. Brick walls, a lot of windows, about five stories high so not too tall, surrounded by lots of green trees on a quiet street off NW Kearney in Nob Hill.

What was surprising was that it was *an apartment building* and not a house.

"You said you had a house," she said, very evenly, to her leopard shifter mate. This was supposedly his house. This was the first time she'd seen it. And this was…not at all what she'd been expecting.

"It used to be a house," he said mildly. "We tore it down and replaced it with the apartment building so it would blend in with the neighborhood better once things here started to change."

"Uh huh." She blinked at the lovely glass front door, the pains covered in dark film so you couldn't see much of the lobby. "You guys couldn't just…I don't know. Move."

He chuckled. Which wasn't a fair move on his part because it danced along her spine like fireworks and made her toes curl in her sensible low heels.

For all they'd been together for a little over three months now, this was the first time she'd seen his home. They always stayed at her little cottage house, ostensibly because she had three dogs and she didn't want to leave them alone for long periods of time. At least that was his explanation for why she hadn't seen his "house" yet. But he'd promised to show her so she'd know he wasn't deliberately keeping her away.

She might have preferred a little forewarning of what to expect though.

"Is the whole apartment building your…home?"

"I have the top floor." Again said so casually. "Caitlin has the third floor mostly to herself."

Caitlin was his younger sister and the other Jones sibling who lived in Portland, working with Deacon on their family business. Which was rescuing animals. Which was how she'd know she was in deep trouble when she met Deacon. How was a woman supposed to resist a man who rescued animals for a living?

Cary had gotten to know Caitlin a bit, so it was comforting to know she'd be here today. This wasn't just a normal boyfriend-showing-her-his-home kind of evening. The entire Jones clan was descending on the place for dinner. They'd just finished their big charity ball, one of their largest fundraising events of the year, and things hadn't exactly gone to plan thanks to the whole cougar shifter thing, so they'd cancelled the family dinner they traditionally had the night after the ball.

Deacon had convinced them to move the dinner up here to Portland instead of him and Cary having to make another trip down to Eugene. She'd initially been grateful for that. At least here, she was in her own territory, so to speak, and she could run away and hide in her own house to if things got weird. Staying with Deacon and his family in their *mansion* leading up to the charity event had been eye opening. And intimidating. And overwhelming. And complicated. All of which meant she had mixed feelings about this dinner.

Her feelings had just gotten even more mixed staring up at the apartment building.

"You told Jon—" a kid she'd had to protect not long after she'd met Deacon— "that you had a house in Nob Hill. Not an *apartment building.*"

"I still call this place my house a lot. Old habits." He shrugged.

As if that explanation excused mixing up a house for an entire building.

"Who lives on the other floors if you and Caitlin take up two?"

"The second and fourth floors are space for leopards living in Portland who don't have their own homes yet, if they've just moved or are between places. Sherri stayed here for a few years after she started her construction business, to save money for the business."

She'd met Sherri during another misadventure with a demon god. And then again down in Eugene for the charity ball. She really liked the older woman but she hadn't had a lot of time to get to know her. Sherri was busy running a business. Cary kept having to save the world. Those kinds of things really cut into socializing time.

"You didn't charge her?"

"We use the extra space as…a haven for our people if they need it. So no, no rents."

"That's nice," she said, nudging him with her shoulder because if she looked at him she might lose herself in his golden eyes and get all distracted by lust.

Her mate was shockingly gorgeous and she was still adjusting to just looking at him. Sometimes she got busy or worried and forgot the impact he could have on her. But then he'd smile, or laugh, or just stand there looking gorgeous and smelling yummy, and she'd melt. The whole thing was pretty disconcerting. She was still getting used to being a mate. Getting used to the fact that he'd told her he loved her.

Speaking of melting.

He used her nudge as an excuse to wrap his arm around her waist and pull her close. She couldn't bring herself to object. Mostly because she didn't want to.

"They're my people. I'll be their leader one day. I want to be able to take care of them."

Yeah, that was the other thing she still hadn't gotten used to yet. Deacon's mother was essentially the queen of the leopard shifters in the Pacific Northwest. And Deacon, being the oldest, would one day take over and be their king. As his mate, she'd also be their leader even if she wasn't a shifter, was in fact a perfectly ordinary human woman —when she wasn't protecting people with magic her bosses had given her—and had no idea how to be a leader of anyone.

Okay, she was the head dog in her little dog pack, but that was really only because Buck and Pickles allowed it. Buck, Labrador by day, demon dog by…well usually never, but it was there in his nature, had been with her since he was a puppy, and he was perfectly happy to look to her to be the boss. Pickles had joined them a few months later. She mostly went about looking like an ordinary, adorable basset hound. But she was actually a retired foo lion whose other form was capable of serious guard duty. Pickles let Cary be the boss too, though. Only her mundane mutt, Fred, the terrier-collie cross, had to be convinced Cary was *always* in charge. Fortunately, Fred could be persuaded to admit Cary's authority so long as there were dog biscuits involved.

She blinked back to her surroundings. "Your family is waiting for us, aren't they?"

"They're expecting us soon, yes. But my mother knows I'm here so we can take our time."

His mother. The *queen* of the leopards. Cary had only just learned that Deacon wasn't an ordinary shifter. And not just because he would one day lead the leopards. He had actual magic. He could do things most other leopard shifters couldn't do. And he got that from his mother. Who could also do magic and a lot of things other shifters couldn't do. Some of that stuff was pretty terrifying.

Deacon didn't use his magic, though. Which was a bone of contention between him and his mother. An argument Cary had no intention of getting in the middle of.

One of their particular abilities, which wasn't common in leopard shifters, was their ability to sense where all their people were within a certain range. Maria Jones had known exactly where Deacon was the minute they were within range of each other. And while they couldn't exactly speak to each other telepathically, Deacon and his mother had an uncanny, unspoken way of communicating.

That might have freaked her out more if she didn't already have so many other things to worry about.

The fact that Maria seemed to like her was good. It didn't make the woman any less intimidating. But at least Cary wasn't worried about her actively trying to end Cary and Deacon's relationship.

"Are you ready?" Deacon asked. "Or would you like to stare up at the building for a bit longer? We have time. They'll wait."

She scowled up at him. A mistake since she got all caught up in his eyes and his mouth and how much fun it would be to kiss him. And maybe drag him back to her place for a little alone time.

His brows lowered and a very faint growl filled the air around them. "I wouldn't object to anything you're thinking right now," he murmured, leaning down to put his mouth close to hers. The hot brush of his breath made her shiver. "But my family will notice if we leave right after arriving. And they'll wonder what happened."

Her eyes widened. She didn't want to explain to his *mother* that she'd dragged Deacon off for sexy times. Yes, mates were apparently insatiable and everyone up there would understand. Still, it was embarrassing to have people know what you were doing when it came to things like sex, so she swallowed down her lust.

"Let's go in."

She straightened away from him and pulled her beat up leather jacket back into place. Then she ran a hand down her slacks. She hadn't dressed up a lot, because Deacon had insisted this was a casual dinner. But she couldn't face Maria's elegance without at least trying for something dressier than her usual jeans and t-shirt. The black dress pants and button up, long sleeve shirt, were the best she could do. And since the shirt was one of her best friend Marianne's magic shirts, complete with the ability to seal bleeding wounds, it seemed a smart choice for a dinner with shapeshifters.

"Ready," she said, taking a deep, fortifying breath.

She ignored Deacon's quiet chuckle as he held the front door for her and she stepped into the lobby.

*L*ike the outside of the building, the lobby was lovely. Polished black marble floors, wooden accents, a switchback set of stairs near the rear of the entryway with deccrative wrought iron railings. The overhead lighting was bright but soft, probably to accommodate shifter eyes. There were two elevators to the left and a single elevator to the right, with a row of only a dozen or so mailboxes just inside the door.

Deacon guided her to the elevator on the right. "Private to my place," he said.

She tried not to roll her eyes. Of course he had a private elevator. Having a rich boyfriend was proving weird but interesting. Especially because she often forgot he had money until he said things like "private elevator."

The interior of the little box was carpeted, which for some reason surprised her, but when she stepped inside and there was no sound of clicking shoes on marble, the carpet made more sense. While Deacon could move insanely quietly over most surfaces, he had very sensitive hearing and so not having to deal with extra, unnecessary sounds probably appealed to him.

They stepped out of the elevator into an entryway. No door to get into an apartment, just straight into the place as if the elevator door was the front door. That abrupt entrance was so far outside her experience of life, Cary stumbled over the threshold.

"Wow," she muttered, taking in her surroundings. She had expected luxury and expensive things because his family's *mansion* was filled with luxury and some expensive things, but the mansion was also a haven for all the leopards and so had very comfortable, casual spaces too. The library in the mansion had been a joyously comfortable room, and her favorite in the house.

Deacon's home was...

The only word she could think of was austere. As austere as his room back at the mansion. His excuse for that was that he didn't spend a lot of time there. And he had bad memories of the room from growing up, when he'd gone through the leopard equivalent of puberty and his magic had caused him a lot of issues. It wasn't exactly a pleasant room for him to stay in anymore, so he hadn't bothered to do much with it.

But judging by his current home, she was now more inclined to think he just didn't consider...softening his surroundings to be a priority. From the elevator, a black marble floor spread out into a huge, high ceilinged living room—so much for worrying about the clicking of shoes on marble. To her left, a closet door and a black lacquered table with a keys bowl and a mail tray were the only things in the entryway.

The living room had a large, L-shaped sofa in dark gray with a glass coffee table placed in the crook of the L. There was a huge TV on one wall, and two shelves of books bracketing the TV—the books were the most personal thing in the room. The walls were a pale, almost white gray with no art decorating them. There were no family pictures on the shelves. No rugs or carpets to pad the marble floors. A bank of large windows gave the room lots of bright winter evening light and there was plenty of beautiful greenery to be seen outside over the tops of other buildings. But no plants in his living room. No pops of color or living things to cut through the starkness.

He took her leather jacket and hung it in the closet next to the elevator. Then motioned her inside. To the right, past the bookshelves and TV, a large, wide, doorless arch opened into what seemed to be a dining area. And that's where she spotted the first signs of life.

Lots of life.

Cary balked. So instinctively she only noticed she'd stopped in her tracks and hesitated to move closer to that dining room when Deacon leaned close and whispered, "Don't worry. They won't bite."

"Ha," she muttered. She still had to force herself forward.

She'd met Caitlin before of course, and she'd met Deacon's twin brother Michael. And she'd seen other members of his family at the charity ball. But there were a lot of siblings and she'd somehow never managed to meet most of them during all the mayhem of the event and the weird stuff that surrounded it. Now faced with all those Joneses, in a setting she was only just seeing for the first time even though it was her mate's home, her gut churned and tossed with nerves.

When Deacon had said the family would come down here for this dinner, she'd been relieved it would at least be in familiar surroundings. But suddenly, this felt a lot less like home ground.

She swallowed down her anxiety, knowing they'd all smell it anyway with their super shifter sense of smell. She straightened her shoulders and tried to smile when they stepped under the arch and into the dining room.

Every eye in the place turned to face them.

Deacon's hand on her back was the only thing that kept her from bolting back to the elevator, for which she was grateful. Running away would be embarrassing.

Also potentially dangerous since the room was full of predators.

The space was as large as the living room, with a giant, long, polished wooden table taking up the center. The black marble floor and pale gray walls continued in here, as well as the theme of no carpets, rugs, or softening accents. Two hanging wrought iron lamps over the tables were turned off, the room filled with late afternoon light from another bank of large windows. Across the table was second wide arch leading into a huge, glossy kitchen. From what she could see, it looked filled with shiny chrome appliances and gray countertops.

Where the hell was the color in this place? It really needed a pop of red or something.

Around the table milled what seemed to be a hundred leopard shifters, but which was in fact only a little over a dozen people. According to Deacon, for this dinner only the immediate Jones family were involved—no mates, partners, aunts, uncles, or kids—to keep from overwhelming Cary. She was still overwhelmed, but probably less than she might have been with even more people to face.

Maria Jones, Deacon's mother, the family matriarch, and the queen of the Pacific Northwest leopard shifters, gave an elegant nod to Cary from her place at the head of the long table. Maria was a beautiful woman, her coloring very similar to Deacon's down to the golden eyes and black hair. It was obvious she was related to Deacon, though when Cary had first seen her, she'd assumed the woman was one of Deacon's sisters. Shifters didn't age exactly the same way as humans, so Deacon didn't look his age either—he was fifty-four but looked in his mid-thirties and by shifter biology standards, that was his equivalent-to-human stage of life. Maria had small creases beside her eyes and a little furrow between her brows, but no other signs of age. She barely looked to be in her late forties.

Her husband and mate, Evan Jones sat to her right. Evan was as tall and broadly build as his son, and it was obvious in his features where Deacon got his looks. Evan's blue eyes contrasted with his dark lashes and hair handsomely, his paler skin tone reflected his Welsh and Scottish ancestry. He was a powerful shifter but didn't possess the magic his son and mate did and so didn't have to be as controlled. He'd been quite friendly and relaxed with her at first, and had even learned to make pizzas for her since Deacon had told him that was her favorite food.

But she and Evan had gotten into a little…tiff. She'd accidently stepped on a delicate topic with regards to Maria and pushed one of Evan's buttons without meaning too. He'd in turn given her one hell of a guilt trip and implied she was bad at her job, which touched on one of her insecurities and pushed her buttons in turn. They'd exchanged apologies since, and were supposedly on good terms again, but they hadn't really had a chance to talk since the apologies. She was still nervous around him, afraid of saying the wrong thing again.

The rest of the room was filled with sisters and brothers that all bore a strong family resemblance to each other, with varying shades of hair color, mostly black to dark brown, and eye colors that ranged from gold through hazel to blue like Evan's. Though they hadn't been introduced yet, Cary recognized Deacon's twin sister Jocelyn immediately by her remarkably strong resemblance to Deacon and Michael. She had brown hair a few shades lighter than Deacon's but the golden eyes that were a match for his and Maria's. Her skin tone was a little darker than Deacon's, and she was as tall as both her twin brothers, making her several inches over six foot tall. She was all lean muscle and graceful gestures, and Cary was more terrified of meeting—and not getting along with—Jocelyn than she was any of his other siblings.

She spotted Caitlin, a study in Jones gorgeousness with her dark brown hair and brown eyes just hinting at gold, with three of the other siblings. Caitlin was closer to Cary's height, and had the kind of figure and face that tended to stop people in their tracks. She gave Cary a friendly wave and detached herself from the others, hurrying over to take Cary's hands.

"It's so good to see you! I'm so sorry we didn't get to talk more at the ball. That was a crazy night, huh?"

"Uh. Yeah." Cary had had to protect leopard kids from a cougar attack and then been kidnapped by Deacon's ex-girlfriend so, yeah, a crazy night.

Though, weirdly, not the craziest of her life.

That probably wasn't a good thing.

"I'm glad we could do this," Caitlin said, then leaned in for a cheek kiss and whispered, "They'll love you. Don't worry. They're already pretty impressed with you."

"Uhm." What did she say to that?

Caitlin swung back to the room and started making the introductions, which bemused Cary since this was Deacon's home. But Caitlin was the more gregarious sibling of the two. Better at "schmoozing" according to Deacon.

"Where's Michael?" Cary asked just before being introduced to Jocelyn.

"He's running late," Caitlin said, with a little sigh. "Got caught at the clinic first thing this morning and then in traffic on his way up. He'll be here soon."

Michael was a vet and ran the animal clinic near the family home outside of Eugene. At one point in her life, Cary had been a vet tech and considered becoming a vet herself, but the work, especially having to put beloved pets to sleep, had hurt too much. She'd been in the middle of rethinking that career path when Jaxer, her faery mentor, and the Nags had entered her life and turned it upside down with this Protector stuff. Her career history, however, had given her a lot to talk about with Michael and had made their initial meeting so much easier.

When they'd worked through the group and finally made their way to Jocelyn, Cary held her breath. Jocelyn might work on the opposite coast, but she was still Deacon's *twin* sister. If she and Cary didn't get along, that would be bad.

Jocelyn offered her hand and a faint smile when Caitlin introduced them. "Pleasure," she said, her voice low and beautifully husky. She shook Cary's hand with just a little pressure and released at an appropriate interval that was neither too abrupt nor too extended. She gave the same faint smile of greeting to her twin. "You're both well?"

"Great," Cary said, not entirely sure how to answer that. "Little hungry."

Caitlin laughed. "We're always hungry. You fit right in."

Jocelyn responded to her younger sister's laugh and comment with another faint smile and a brief nod. But the smiles all looked forced. Like she would prefer not to be here having this conversation. Cary might have taken that personally but for the distant look in Jocelyn's gaze even when she looked at her siblings.

Cary tried to gage Deacon's expression from the corner of her eye, wishing for just a moment she had his sense of smell so she could tell what he was feeling and thinking. He could relax around his family, not have to exert the kind of control he did around other leopards, so he wasn't the ice man he became in the middle of large numbers of his people, but he was still hard to read in moments like this. She would have loved to know if he sensed an issue with this sister or was this just the way Jocelyn always was with everyone. Although, she supposed if she had his sense of smell, she'd be able to judge Jocelyn better herself and wouldn't need clues from Deacon. Caitlin didn't seem to notice anything, though, so maybe Jocelyn was just a very reserved person.

"You weren't injured during that…incident with Sasha?" Jocelyn asked.

There was a pause around the room. Subtle, but there. As if everyone had collectively held their breaths and were trying to listen to Cary's answer without making it obvious they were listening. Since they were all shifters and could hear a pin drop two rooms away, the drama seemed a bit excessive to her.

"Nope," she said. "Just fine."

She'd picked up some cuts and bruises and one hell of a knot to the back of the head when Sasha had kidnapped her. But thanks to her Protector magic, she was able to heal faster than the average human and had recovered from that all pretty quickly once she got home and got to sleep. Healing sleeps had become a regular part of her life since taking up this job, a job she felt wholly unqualified for even after more than six years. She sort of enjoyed the long sleeps now, though. They were refreshing.

None of that was anything she figured Jocelyn wanted to know. And the rest of the waiting room didn't need to know. Maria had seen her, known her injuries. If they wanted that gossip, they could ask their mother. Or Deacon for that matter.

Jocelyn gave her a slow blink and another faint smile. "I'm glad. I've never really liked Sasha."

Cary raised her brows. That was more blunt than she'd been expecting. "I got the impression Michael doesn't either," she said, testing the water.

"He doesn't." She flicked a glance at Deacon. "We noticed things other people didn't."

Well. If Cary had to guess, she'd say Deacon's sister had just scolded him for being an unobservant idiot in the most subtle and soft way possible. That was interesting.

"Are you able to stay a little longer before getting back to Boston?" Deacon asked, in what seemed like a subject change, but not as if he was rushing her back to her coast. He actually sounded like he hoped she stay around longer.

Also interesting.

"Wish I could," she said. She did not sound like she was interested in hanging out on this coast much longer. "I had to leave some work unfinished. That'll bother me until I get it sorted out."

"Fair enough," Deacon said on a sigh. "You should visit more."

"You sound like mother."

"She has a point."

"If you say so."

Cary tried not to let her head ping pong back and forth as she witnessed this exchange like an eager audience member at a tennis match. But the little insight into their family dynamic, and more importantly, how the twins dealt with each other was fascinating.

"Let me introduce you to our youngest sister and brother," Caitlin said, taking Cary's arm to lead her away. Leaving Deacon behind with Jocelyn.

"I take it they had something to discuss and I needed to be distracted so they could," Cary said under her breath to Caitlin.

Caitlin let out a little puff of air. "We're not very subtle are we? Yes, there's stuff going on there. He'll tell you later I'm sure, if it comes up. But Jocelyn is having a hard time lately. Long story. Deacon and Michael are worried about her."

Curiouser and curiouser, Cary thought as she forced herself *not* to look over her shoulder and study Deacon and his twin.

"Julia come here," Caitlin called. "Dylan."

A young man and woman turned their heads almost in unison even though they were talking with two different groups.

Julia had been chatting with her father and mother. She jumped up from the table and trotted close, hand outstretched to shake Cary's hand even before she'd reached them. She was shorter than most of the other sisters, closer to Maria's height, but had dyed her short hair blonde which suited the blue eyes she'd inherited from her father rather well. From what Caitlin had told her, Julia was a chemist who worked in pharmaceuticals research, and had developed some interesting drugs for the family business—with occasional shifter twists.

Dylan was a lot taller than Julia, but not quite as tall as Deacon. He matched his twin's blue eyes with light brown hair that had flashes of red in it. Caitlin had mentioned in passing that Dylan was an astronomer in training, which Cary found pretty exciting since her best friend Angie was an amateur astronomer, too.

He ambled over slower than Julia but shook Cary's hand with equal enthusiasm. "Great to finally meet you," he said.

"Oh yes," Julia said. "I've heard so much! I've been so excited to meet you. The kids say you're a superhero."

Cary coughed and raised her hands. "No. No. Not a superhero. Just… Not a superhero." It was one thing for the leopard shifter kids to make that leap—and for her to pretend in her head because it was fun—but another thing all together for Deacon's siblings to consider her a superhero.

Maria knew Cary was a Protector, but for her own safety, Cary didn't tell people *what* she was most of the time. She'd slipped with Deacon the first time they'd met, which should have clued her in that he wasn't her normal protectee. But Maria had kept the secret, allowing Cary the space to decide if she'd tell the Jones clan the whole truth.

And frankly, she hadn't decided if she would or not yet. The fewer people who knew, the safer she was. Lately, it had started to feel like way too many people already knew, so part of her wanted to prevent any remaining slips. Even if that meant keeping most of Deacon's family in the dark.

Hardly a way to ensure trust, she supposed. But for now, she kept her actual job description to herself.

So she switched the topic. "I was kind of wondering why your parents echoed the 'J' and 'D' names for you two. Was that ever confusing? Deacon, Dylan. Jocelyn, Julia?"

Julia rolled her eyes. "If we'd had another sibling, they would have been saddled with an 'M' name, too. Mom has a really weird sense of humor and aesthetic. She knew we'd be her last kids and wanted the… symmetry. Start her kids with J, D, and M names, end her kids with J, D, and M names."

"Because…symmetry?" Cary shrugged. "Okay. But why J, D, and M? Do those have significance?"

"Not that Mom's ever admitted to us," Dylan said with a charmingly crooked smile. "She claims the oldest got their names because she and Dad liked them. Julia and I got stuck with alternatives for Mom's amusement."

"Could have been worse," Julia said with a philosophical shrug. "Some of the Welsh names Dad suggested had so many vowels I'd have been forever correcting people on the spelling."

Dylan chuckled. "I was going to be Meilyr." He spelled it out. "A nice name, but yeah, I'd have to correct spelling mistakes a lot."

"Why did you end up a 'D' instead?" Cary asked, finding the whole thing ridiculously fascinating.

Maria and Evan had had to name fourteen children. That struck Cary as a lot of coming up with names. Her sister had three kids and she'd picked names according to how they sounded combined with her husband's last name. Cary remembered Valerie mentioning combing through baby books for months, but it hadn't occurred to Cary how complicated the process might be. She'd named pets before, the ones that hadn't named themselves, but she'd never thought about naming kids.

The conversation was diverting enough, she forgot to be uncomfortable and uneasy around all the strangers. Caitlin had a gift for facilitating conversation too, and Julia and Dylan were chatting and friendly. They moved from names to Dylan's work, to Julia's research, and had segued to discussing food, a favorite topic of Cary's, by the time Deacon joined them.

"Everything okay?" she asked with a little sideways look at him.

He nodded. But didn't say more.

Okay. Well, she'd ask later.

Caitlin pulled her cellphone from her back pocket when it pinged and checked the screen. "Oh good. Michael's here. Just parking the car. He'll be up soon." She looked up from her phone. "Finally, we can eat!"

That news was met by a resounding cheer.

3

The food was an excellent mashup of dishes provided by everyone in the family. Deacon supplied the wine, drinks and location. He was as indifferent to cooking as Cary even though he loved food as much as she did. Maria didn't spend much time cooking either. But Evan was a budding amateur chef, and managed to pull off a truly great main course of coq au vin that made Cary rethink her relationship with chicken. He also served up a huge tub of bangers and mash and the combination of hearty English sausage with fancy French chicken was probably her favorite thing about the meal.

And boy was there a lot of meal. Each sibling contributed at least two dishes and each dish was enough to feed a small army. But given they were a family of shapeshifters who had to eat a lot to keep up with their metabolisms, the quantities seemed appropriate.

Though even Cary's significant appetite was pushed to its limits as more and more emerged from the kitchen. Roasted winter vegetables, soups packed with flavor, savory bread puddings, cheeses, breads, a fish dish she passed on, rolls packed with meat and sauce and cheese, an eggplant lasagna from Jocelyn that tasted like heaven. Michael brought the desserts and Cary's sweet-tooth nearly exploded with the joy of so many cakes and pastry options. Evan made homemade ice cream to just gild the lily.

By the time they'd settled down into the last courses of cheese and dessert and coffee, Cary was more full than any holiday she'd ever experienced and figured she could probably sleep for a week in this food coma. She hadn't had to make much conversation. The siblings spent an inordinate amount of time ribbing each other, reminiscing, and arguing politics—which surprised her for some reason; she didn't think of shifters as being all that interested in human politics. They talked about the business, and about their work if it wasn't part of the family business.

They *didn't* discuss the cougar shifters or the negotiation going on between Maria and the cougars to reestablish their peace settlement. Once the cougars' "inside man" was discovered, and they no longer had that advantage, their more violent impulses toward the leopards had eased off. Many of the cougars still wanted to be the top shifters in the area, but Maria wasn't the kind of queen any of them could compete with. And after so many failures and the leopards having captured a number of their people, the cougars were at least at the table for a peace settlement.

Cary knew all this from Deacon, but the family very conspicuously avoided the topic during the meal. She'd ask him about that later. Likely, no one wanted to discuss the fact that they'd been betrayed by one of their own.

Cary sipped her coffee, leaning back in the surprisingly comfortable chairs surrounding Deacon's table—she'd expected them to be stiff and uncomfortable given the décor in his place—and listened to the roll of conversation around her, enjoying the rhythms of clamorous chatter while she sat in a quiet bubble with a steaming cup of delectable coffee.

She was considering if she might be able to stuff in one more petit fours, because they were both delicious and small enough she could pretend it wasn't one bite too far, when a too familiar sensation crawled along her spine. The sensation that warned her...

Her bosses needed her.

Shit. She'd hoped she'd manage to get the whole night off. But she was in a test year now, her seventh year as a Protector, when she had to prove that she could do this job without the help of her mentor. She either survived or died, and she did it on her own. The test year meant she couldn't refuse any jobs her bosses sent her way. Even though she'd have liked to have refused a few of the recent ones. And since *they'd* made a mistake on one of her jobs while she'd been at the Jones mansion, they'd been more irritable than normal.

Well, Liruk was always irritable. It was just worse now.

She excused herself, feigning a trip to the bathroom so Deacon wouldn't feel the need to follow her, and moved out into the living room, attempting to get as far away from the dining room as possible. Not that she stood a chance of keeping secrets from shifters with excellent hearing. Still, she could try not to disturb their celebration with her job interruption.

But even though she expected Wisat and Liruk to appear as they always did when she got this sensation, nothing happened. She stood in the living room for several long moments just waiting.

"Where are you two?" she murmured very quietly. No one answered.

Frowning, she went back to the dining room and whispered to Deacon, "I need to step outside. Wisat and Liruk are around here somewhere, but they aren't appearing in your living room."

Deacon sighed. "I'll go with you."

"No! If you get up and leave, your family will know something is wrong. I don't want to disturb their party."

"I'm coming with you. I'm still not…good after what happened. I don't dare stay here without you around."

That was his first hint that even being with his family worried him given the state of his control. He'd told her they had some level of natural protection from his magic. And with Maria here to help control him if he did start to slip, it hadn't occurred to Cary that there was much to worry about leaving him alone.

Apparently, she'd been wrong.

He had been even more attached to her since his ex had kidnapped and tried to kill her. Since his control slipped so much he'd nearly killed some of his own people, including his ex. Cary had not enjoyed having to protect Sasha from Deacon since Sasha was a bitch. She'd prefer never having to protect a bad guy from Deacon again. The whole thing had left him shaky, and he hadn't wanted to risk being away from her much. The whole thing had shaken her too, so she hadn't wanted to be away from him much either.

It had only been a week since he'd lost control so thoroughly. She understood his hesitance. But work was work. She had to go. And if he had to go with her…

"Give your family an excuse that won't worry them," she murmured. The tingle along her spine intensified, almost as if her bosses were impatiently nudging her. There was a reason she called them the Nags. "I'll head downstairs and you can meet me."

She hurried out, trying to remain inconspicuous about it. Given the loud conversation going on around the table as the family debated a topic she'd missed and so couldn't follow, she hoped no one would even notice she was gone.

Deacon joined her at the elevator just as it pinged open.

"What did you tell them?" she asked after the doors had closed and they'd gone down one floor, ensuring they weren't overheard. She was pretty sure this whole building was sound proofed since only shifters lived here, but better to be safe.

"That you had to take a call downstairs for privacy from shifter hearing," he said. "One of your friends."

"Good. Not worrying. What did you tell them about coming with me?"

"I didn't have to explain that."

That was…maybe not good. And definitely worrying. She took his hand and squeezed.

The elevator opened onto the lobby and Cary was heading for the front door of the building when Deacon pulled her to a stop. He nodded behind him, to the building stairs. She turned, and the Nags stepped out from the shadows.

"Why did you make me come down here?" she asked, maybe a little too sharply.

Wisat gave her a strange look. "We wouldn't invade your mate's privacy by entering his home without first being invited."

"We have some manners," Liruk said.

Cary wasn't so sure about that, but… "Fine. What's up?" She tried to judge the situation from their expressions but that was always a futile attempt.

Wisat and Liruk were members of the North American Fae who made Protectors. They were shockingly gorgeous but in a way that was very Fae and very not human. Wisat, with his black robes, cherry red skin, and black silk hair had two intertwining red velvet-covered antlers forming a halo on his head. Liruk was gold and white to Wisat's black and red. Her white hair hung to the ground over her white robe, her golden skin only one shade darker than the golden horns that emerged from her hair at the top of her head. They both had eyes so green they glowed, and she'd never been entirely sure if that was coincidence, a familial trait—Wisat and Liruk had never mentioned being related but who knew with Fae—or just common for their species.

They popped in and out of her life on a regular basis to give her assignments, and they paid her salary. She sort of even liked them because they tried to help stop at least some of the bad things that happened in the world. But their timing was notoriously rotten.

"Have you finished with your meal?" Wisat asked, because he was the one who cared about those sorts of things. Liruk didn't think Cary's personal life should ever interfere with her job. Or even be a part of the equation when it came to doing her job.

"We've eaten," she said. Technically the meal wasn't over, but she couldn't have eaten more if she'd wanted to. Well, except for maybe that one last petit fours.

"Good because you have a job," Liruk said, her tone pinched and a little sharper even than usual.

Cary frowned at her. "You want to tell me what it is or are you just going to stand there glaring at me?"

Wisat gave Liruk a raised brow look and Liruk pressed her lips together and looked away, not meeting Wisat's gaze.

Huh. That was interesting. Were they fighting? She'd never seen them look even remotely put out with each other. And wow, did her curiosity surge. So many questions. The willpower necessary to *not* ask any of those questions was epic, and she felt very proud of that effort.

Because Liruk was right, if they were here, she had a job to do. Someone was in danger.

"There's an issue not far from here. With Deacon's help you should manage the distance without driving." Wisat glanced at Deacon who nodded in answer to the unspoken question.

The fact that her bosses were just assuming Deacon would be going with her on her job during a test year, and even encouraging him to help her do her job, was…odd. But she wasn't going to argue. Even in Protector mode she couldn't run as fast as Deacon.

"A young couple will be accosted by…something," Liruk said.

"Something? You don't have more than that for me?"

They didn't always know what the bad guy would be. Most of their part of this job involved spotting trouble through premonitions and research, but the way Liruk said "something" made Cary think they were more in the dark than usual. And they never admitted that to her so obviously.

"Get to the couple and protect them," Wisat said. He gave the location, an address near Lower Macleary Park. "The younger of the two men will one day be a great wizard. A good man who will accomplish great things. It's important he and his mate are not killed."

Wow. "Okay." She headed toward the door in a hurry, Deacon close behind.

Not all of her jobs involved protecting "important" people. Often they were just ordinary people in the wrong place at that wrong time. But occasionally, the protectee had a potential fate or future that could be snuffed out if not kept safe in a very specific moment. Those particular jobs always caused her a little extra layer of anxiety, a heightened sense that failure—something she always feared with this job—would have even more dire consequences beyond just the loss of a living being.

She'd already pushed open the lobby's front door, when the sound of the elevators behind her made her turn.

Deacon's family emerged from all three elevators at once. Every single sibling as well as Maria and Evan converged on the lobby. Liruk and Wisat had vanished.

"What's happening?" Maria asked.

Cary tried not to panic. "Nothing. We're good. Just… Gotta go do a thing." She met Maria's gaze and tried to convey more than she could say aloud. Maria knew her job, she had to know this wasn't something the whole family needed to help with.

"You're worried," Caitlin said. "Is it something bad? Your friend?"

"Nope. Just gotta go. Sorry to leave so fast. You guys enjoy the rest of the dessert. Save me a petit fours." She jumped into Deacon's arms so he could run with her and murmured against his ear, "Hurry."

She didn't wait to see what the Joneses did. The urge to reach her charge was overwhelming her now. The urgency driving her hard, her nerves alight with anxiety. Danger was closing in on the couple, faster than she'd thought would happen. Her Protector senses pushed her.

Her charges needed her. Now.

4

The cul-de-sac was filled with small, cozy houses that probably cost a fortune because of their location even though they looked like everyday, ordinary homes in a variety of styles. Trees and hilly front yards covered with easy maintenance greenery mixed with houses closer to the sidewalk with neatly mowed lawns. The cold winter air smelled like woodsmoke and a dampness that hinted of rain. Street lights gave the road a quiet, peaceful feel that belied Cary's urgency.

She took a beat to settle her stomach as she studied their surroundings. Running at shifter speeds, even with her eyes closed, always left her faintly motion sick.

Fully dark but still early enough in the evening, most of the homes had their lights blazing. Cars moved down the cross road behind them, but this street was quiet and relatively empty. She heard the TV on in the house right next to them. Otherwise not a lot of movement. The street dead-ended at the edge of Lower Macleary Park, and the forest flowed down to the very edge of the road, touching the last houses' property lines.

She scanned the street, hunting for her charges.

There.

Two young men, maybe mid-twenties though she had trouble telling in the dark, hand in hand, their full attention on each other as they ambled down the block. One laughed and the other grinned down at him, looking very pleased with his partner's reaction. They seemed happy and at ease. It was difficult to tell if they were just out for a walk or headed home, but that hardly mattered.

Because beyond them, just coming out of the woods, crept something Cary had never encountered in all her years as a Protector.

A monster.

An honest-to-god monster.

Not a vampire, or werewolf, or shifter of any kind, or even a demon. No human-shaped evil being at all.

A monster.

This one had the head of an octopus, with eyes all over its rounded head—lots and lots of eyes—and a huge mouth filled with very very sharp, gleaming, dripping teeth. Its body was a combination of tentacles and lizard-like clawed feet, at least six of those lizard feet and legs sticking out from the huge, bulbous body. The tentacles were covered in suction cups, but the cups were flexing as the tentacles moved, and Cary could swear there were teeth inside those disks. The body was more like a lizard's, thick and low to the ground, covered in tiny plate-like armor that chinked as the creature moved. Some feathers, which looked incongruous, stuck out from its backside like a plume, but that bit of finery did nothing to take away from the overall horror of what she was seeing.

As the creature slithered—slithered!—closer to the men, it let out a quiet sound similar to insect chittering that scratched across her nerves like nails on a chalkboard, making the hairs on her arms and the back of her neck stand up.

She didn't even have to ask Deacon, he moved so fast the world around her blurred, and the next moment, she was standing between the monster and all three men.

"What the…?" one of the men started.

"Just stay behind me," she said. "I can keep you safe, but you have to stay there."

"What are you talking about?" the other man said.

She glanced back. Deacon was standing behind and just to her right, half blocking the two men himself. One of her two charges was maybe her height, an inch or two taller, but was older than she'd at first assumed. Closer to early thirties than twenties, with a chiseled-jaw, brown-haired, blue-eyed look that belonged on magazine covers.

The younger of the two men was taller than his partner and lankier, but equally as handsome, with hair and eyes a deep brown, almost black. His hair cut into a short, straight style that fluffed a little at the top and reminded Cary vaguely of one of her friend Lucy's favorite K-Pop singers. In the soft, yellow street light, the younger man looked pale and there were circles under his eyes, a sign of tiredness belied by his earlier cheer.

The men had taken a step back at Cary and Deacon's sudden appearance, and the older one was looking around as if hunting for an escape.

"Listen, I know this is a bit abrupt," she said, raising her hands in a calming gesture, "but if you'll just look over there." She gestured to the monster, which had stopped a few yards away, its multitude of eyes blinking at them as it moved right and left in small, undulating steps, assessing the group.

Both men gasped and one cursed.

"What the hell is that?" the older man said, his voice very deep and resonant. He had the kind of voice that made people pause to listen closer.

"That," Cary said, keeping her own voice calm and as matter-of-fact as possible, "is a monster. And I'm not sure what it's doing here. There are people who usually take care of them. But don't worry, I can keep you safe. You just have to stay behind me and don't try to run away. Okay."

"How?" the younger man stuttered. "How can you keep us safe?"

She waved her hand vaguely. "A knack. You're a wizard, right?"

The young man sucked in a sharp breath. "You can't know that. How do you know that?"

Well, she wasn't going to admit the truth. "Long story. But you understand shields?"

The man shrugged.

"So you get this." She was prevaricating and circling the real answer, but she hoped they didn't notice and ask more questions.

The young wizard opened his mouth to say more, dashing Cary's hope. But he never got his question out.

In that moment, the monster lunged.

It flew through the air with a speed that made even Cary gasp and Deacon curse. Wow. Its tentacles slapped against her shield and stuck to it, the sucking motion and gnashing teeth *inside* the suction cups making a gross sort of kissing sound that made Cary want to gag. The monster's head pressed forward against her shield, its eyes blinking in a strange pattern as its mouth worked in a sort of gulping chomp, stretching toward her face.

The thing was larger than it had seemed coming out of the woods. Up close, it was huge, its head the size of her coffee table, the body stretching out to the size of a small car. Its tentacles flailed overhead, smacking against her shields as it hunted for a way past. When it reared up onto two of its six legs, showing her its belly, she was appalled to see more eyes and another two mouths full of teeth.

The thing had a lot of mouths. And teeth.

Gross.

"I don't usually handle monsters," she said to her charges as she stared in horror at the thing in front of her. She tried to keep that fear from her voice, but the chink chink sound of teeth against teeth made her gut clench. "There are whole families that take care of monsters. Seven families actually."

The creature screeched and it was like something out of a Godzilla movie. Cary winced.

More cursing behind her.

"We have to get out of here," one man said.

"No!"

She spun to face them, trusting her shield to keep the monster at bay even though turning her back on the creature made all the hairs on her body stand up. It was all she could do not to show her own desire to run away. She wasn't the run-away type most of the time. Her instincts tended more toward freeze in place and just...stand there. Which was a handy trait for a Protector. But maybe not such a good survival skill when encountering monsters.

Still, thanks to her magic, she knew the creature couldn't get through her, so she forced herself to keep her back to it in order to ensure her charges didn't do anything stupid.

Like try to run away.

"You notice how it's not getting at us?" she said. "You're safe. Right here. Just so long as you stick close. It can't get to you. But you have to stick close to me."

The older man still looked like he wanted to bolt, his gaze traveling around the area in a frantic search for escape. The younger man's gaze was glued to the monster, transfixed. Though by horror or fascination Cary couldn't tell.

"How about we introduce ourselves," she said. "That might help us all remain calm. I'm Cary. This is my boyfriend Deacon."

Hey! She'd said the word boyfriend without stumbling. That was good. Despite his recent declaration of love, and her returning the feeling even if she hadn't said the words yet, she still stumbled over what to call him. He was her mate in the shifter sense, but she wasn't a shifter. And boyfriend seemed strange because she wasn't used to using it. But the fact that she'd managed it this time without stuttering was definite progress.

"Glen," the older man said, his deep voice giving the name a nice roll. "What are you?" he asked Cary.

"Concerned citizen," she gave her automatic response. "How about you?" she asked the younger man.

"Kevin," he murmured, his gaze still fixed to the monster.

"Why did you call him a wizard?" Glen asked. "That's not a gay slur I've heard before."

Cary made a face. "It wasn't a slur, gay or otherwise." She cut a look to Kevin who'd finally stopped staring at the monster and was focused on the ground now. "Uhm," she said, "I guess I was thinking of someone else."

She winced. That was a really asinine attempt to cover her slip. If she'd known Glen didn't know his boyfriend was a wizard, she wouldn't have said it out loud.

When Kevin glanced up briefly, she mouthed, "Sorry."

He shrugged, but that didn't help Cary feel better.

"Anyway," she said, hoping to distract Glen into forgetting what she'd said about Kevin. "As you can see, we're all safe right now, so we'll just wait here for the monster to get bored and go away."

Not that she wanted to let it just wander back into the woods unchecked. Unfortunately, that was the problem with possessing a purely defensive power, though. She could stand here and keep her charges safe for the rest of the night. But she couldn't do anything about the monster. She didn't have the first clue how to kill one—she hadn't bothered learning how since the Seven Families did the monster hunting—and while her Protector magic would usually give her whatever fighting or weapons skills she needed in the moment, if it helped her keep her charges safe, she didn't have any weapons on her that might aid in killing the monster.

For the most part, she just stood between bad guys and good guys and kept the good guys safe. That was her job. She was a walking Kevlar vest. And Kevlar vests didn't *do* anything.

Under normal circumstances, she could usually irritate a bad guy enough to get them to leave. She had a knack for irritating bad guys. But she couldn't talk her way out of this with a monster. They weren't reasoning creatures. They were… Well, monsters. And this particular one didn't look like it could have a conversation even if it was inclined.

Mostly, it just looked like it wanted to feed.

Gross.

"Plan?" Deacon murmured close to her ear.

"Stand here. Everyone's safe."

"Fair."

She was kind of wishing she'd gotten the phone number of a monster hunter at some point in her life. Angie had given her the contact information for a demon hunter. That was handy. But she'd never faced an actual, horror movie nightmare monster before, so she'd never had call to contact the Seven Families. They obviously did their job really well most of the time. At least in her neck of the woods.

The monster wrapped tentacles all the way around her shields, attempting to reach them from the back. Both Glen and Kevin stepped closer to her, Kevin panting like he might hyperventilate.

"Breathe," she said to him, reaching back to squeeze his arm. "Breathe. You're okay. See. Can't even go around me to get to you."

Kevin gulped in a breath. Then another. Then another.

The sounds of the monster's suction cup mouths sucking and clicking made her teeth tighten, but she focused on Kevin. Rubbing a hand up and down his arm as she kept her gaze mostly on the monster's head, hoping she'd be able to judge its next move.

This was significantly harder with a thing that had multiple eyes on various parts of its body and no discernable cognizance.

When Kevin's breathing sounded normal again, she released his arm and let Glen pull him close, wrapping the taller man in a protective hug.

"We'll be okay," Glen murmured. "We'll be fine."

"Yeah, you will," Cary reassured. "I promise. This thing won't reach you." But boy, could she use some help getting it gone. Maybe dead.

The mouths on its stomach gnashed at her face.

Yeah, dead would be safest.

Where the hell had this thing come from? And why go after a budding wizard who was still keeping his skills a secret from his boyfriend, but who the Nags said would one day do great things? Was that coincidence? Just wrong place wrong time?

It happened, she supposed. But she hated coincidences. They always felt…wrong. Like they weren't and there was some underlying plan.

Could she attribute underlying plans to monsters? Probably not, but still.

"I could try too—" Deacon started.

"No." She didn't even look at him. She pointed her finger at him without taking her attention away from the monster. "You are not attempting to fight and kill a monster with your bare hands I don't care how fast you move. That thing has tentacles with *mouths* on them. This is not up for debate."

She did give him a look then, brief but with a lot of intent. They'd been through enough in the last week. His control and balance were already way off. She did not want him going full angry leopard shifter right now.

"Kinda wishing I'd gotten that gun my father keeps insisting I get," Glen said, his deep voice sounding strained now.

"No telling if a gun would even help," Cary said.

She had a vague memory, from her early years after getting the Protector job when she'd tried to learn everything at once, that monsters needing to have their heads removed or they could just keep coming. That required both knowing which part was the head—she was *pretty* sure the squid-like bulbous part was its head—and having a weapon that could remove heads. A gun with only a few bullets wouldn't do it. And might just irritate an already dangerous creature.

That would be bad.

"And they're dangerous," Kevin said, sounding a lot less likely to hyperventilate now. "I don't want a gun in the house. Not when…if… when the adoption goes through."

"Ah, you guys are adopting?" Cary asked.

"A dog," Glen said, sounding amused. "We're starting with a dog."

Cary grinned. "It's a start. I have three of those myself."

"I love dogs," Kevin said. "And cats. And all animals." He shivered hard enough Cary felt it at her back. "Well, maybe not all animals."

"I'm pretty sure we can count monsters in their own category," Cary said. "Even us animal lovers don't have to love monsters." Especially not monsters trying their damnedest to eat them.

The creature started shuffling back and forth around Cary's shield, its tentacles flailing over their heads as it skittered this way and that, looking for a way closer. A sound like a moan escaped one of its mouths while the others chittered. There was even a buzzing sound just under the chittering.

The combination set her teeth on edge. So much nails-on-chalkboard irritation. Argh.

A tentacle slapped at the shield in front of Cary's face, the sucking suction cups straining to get close. There looked to be something dripping from those little mouths now, a liquid that sizzled when it hit the sidewalk.

Very not good.

She wanted to ask Kevin if he had any wizard tricks up his sleeve. A helpful bolt of lightning or an energy ball or two would be useful. But given his reaction earlier, she didn't dare ask. If he hadn't told Glen yet, it wasn't her place to spill those beans any more than she already had.

They could really really use a wizard bolt about now, though.

The monster reared up on its two back lizard legs and roared again, that Godzilla noise that made Cary wince. Holy hell. It was going to call the attention of every house in the neighborhood. Then she'd have all kinds of innocent bystanders to protect.

And the monster moved fast. What if she didn't get between it and other people in time?

She shoved the fear down. "Shhh," she hissed at the monster. "You're being too loud."

It didn't react to her scolding with so much as a pause in its slapping, flailing attack. Then she felt silly for saying anything. It was a monster, not a typical bad guy she could *talk* to.

It dropped back to its six lizard legs and threw itself at her with a lunge that was so fast it startled a gasp from her. The lunge smacked it up against her shield, flattening the head and making the eyes bulge. The central mouth chittered and scrapped against the invisible barrier.

"We could really use a monster hunter about now," Cary muttered under her breath.

"Will we do?" Caitlin said.

Cary eyes widened. She turned in horror…

To see the entire Jones clan standing behind her.

5

"No!" But Cary's protest came too late, and shifters move too damned fast.

The entire clan descended on the monster, moving at speeds that blurred, hisses and growls filling the cold night air, echoing around the quiet cul-de-sac.

Deacon cursed and then he was gone, too, no longer behind her and safe.

Son of a bitch. She motioned Glen and Kevin closer. "Stay near."

Because of the chaos, she turned and wrapped her arms around the two men, a physical shield she hoped would also prevent them from panicking and trying to run. Or worse, get involved in the fight.

Neither man objected. They held each other and let her hold them, and around them the screeches of a monster out of a horror film meshed with the hisses of big cats.

She tried to watch the fight. Unsuccessfully. The damned monster moved almost as fast as the shifters when it got going. There were flailing tentacles, the skritching of sharp nails, teeth clicking together. A few shouted orders, but mostly the Joneses fought without words. A pack of blurring speed, weaving in and out, around the monster.

Glen cursed when a tentacle landed near his foot—detached from the monster. The suckers continued to flex and move, the limb flopping around. And to Cary's horror, the severed limb jumped and danced toward them, like it had a life of its own, throwing itself at her shields and trying to get through.

Ew.

She tightened her hold on the men, unnecessarily, but it made her feel better. The three of them clung to each other as another severed limb—this time one of the lizard legs—flew above them spraying blood.

A blink and Deacon was next to her again, close enough to be encompassed in her protection. "We're having trouble getting at its head. And the limbs we're pulling off keep fighting."

"Noticed. That's really gross."

He grunted, his gaze on the fight. His eyes glowed yellow now, his shifter nature at the surface. "We need a sword for the head. And a flamethrower. I don't think this thing will stop moving unless we turn it to ash."

"Don't suppose your mother thought to bring a flamethrower to dinner?"

"Nope. No weapons at all this time. Just us."

"We're going to attract an audience soon." She didn't have Jaxer there to glamour the scene and keep innocent people from spotting them. Everyone's cellphone had a video camera. Someone was going to look out a window soon and start recording. If they hadn't already.

"Yup," Deacon said, and before she could say more, he'd blurred away from her, rejoining the fight.

Damn it. She snarled as fear churned through her gut. She knew deep down the Jones family of *shapeshifters* could take care of themselves, but she'd feel better if they'd just let her protect them. She was terrified someone would get hurt. Or worse, killed.

Her gaze landed on Kevin. A wizard. With access to things like fireballs if he'd been studying and practicing.

But since Glen didn't know Kevin was a wizard, had Kevin *been* practicing? How did she ask without outing Kevin before he was ready? She'd already slipped once. She didn't want to cause any harm to their relationship.

But they really really needed some fire about now.

A wizard couldn't help with manifesting swords out of thin air. But they could toss around things that burned.

She met Kevin's wide-eyed gaze. "Flames would be good about now," she said. She didn't look away as his dark eyes widened more.

It was the best she could do without actually asking aloud if he'd studied and used his magic yet. An untrained wizard trying to conjure wizard bolts or flame balls would be as dangerous as the monster. And she wasn't sure how her powers would work in that situation. Would she be able to protect him from himself?

A sharper hiss from her left and a curse that sounded like Caitlin's voice made her look away from Kevin. "You okay?" she called, not sure if anyone would even be able to answer.

"Damned things teeth are sharp," Caitlin said, cursing again. She stopped moving and glared at a little round spot on her forearm, while holding the severed tip of a tentacle in her other hand. The single suction cup on the tentacle was surrounded in blood.

"Get close so I can keep you safe while you heal," Cary called.

Caitlin reacted without question, which sort of surprised Cary since Caitlin didn't know what she was. Caitlin tossed the tentacle tip on the ground and slammed down on it with her foot, which sent blood spraying out beyond Cary's shield. Then Caitlin moved in close enough for Cary's shield to encompass her and keep her safe from the rest of the fight.

"Poison?" Cary asked, frowning down at the wound. It had sealed shut already thanks to super fast shifter healing, but it was still angry red.

"No." Caitlin continued to glare at her arm. "Acid. Burns like a bitch. It'll heal in a minute."

"Who are you people?" Glen asked, his deep voice strained and tight.

"You have a nice voice," Caitlin said instead of answering his question. "Very resonant."

The comment startled a blink from Glen.

By way of distraction, it seemed to work, because by the time Glen opened his mouth to speak again, the angry welt on Caitlin's arm had nearly healed. She tapped Cary on the shoulder. Then blurred into the fight again.

"Who are you?" Glen said again.

"Concerned citizens?" Cary tried.

Glen's look said he knew her excuse was obvious bullshit. She shrugged.

"Fire," Kevin murmured.

Both Cary and Glen looked at him.

"What?" Glen asked.

Kevin met Cary's stare. "You said fire. You need fire."

She nodded.

"Are you carrying a lighter I don't know about?" Glen asked. "You haven't started smoking again, have you?"

The gentle scolding and concern made Cary want to smile.

"No," Kevin said. He faced Glen, holding his gaze. "I never smoked. I said that as an excuse to explain the smell."

Glen frowned.

But Cary got the implication. "You've been practicing," she said. "Training."

Kevin nodded.

"Practicing what?" Glen demanded. "What would you be practicing that made you smell like cigarette smoke? You a secret firefighter and haven't wanted to tell me?"

Why anyone wouldn't admit to that was a mystery to Cary, but for a mundane human, what other excuse would there be? For Glen, that was probably as good a guess as any.

"No," Kevin said, letting out a long breath as he released his hold on Glen, taking a step away from both her and Glen, though still close enough he was well within her protection. "Nothing like that I'm afraid."

He stared out into the fight, the shifting blurs of motion punctuated by the spray of blood as another limb flew from the center of the conflict. The lizard leg dropped a few feet from them, sliding until it stopped against her shield a foot away. The nails scrambled at the ground as the leg attempted to move.

Kevin raised his hand, let out a quiet, resigned breath, and murmured an apology to Glen.

A fireball flared to life on the center of Kevin's upturned palm, the size of a baseball, controlled and tightly bound as it hovered just above his skin. He flexed his fingers, then tossed the fireball, his aim true. It hit the lizard leg dead center and engulfed the limb in bright red and yellow flames. The stench of burning flesh blew over her, making her gag.

A noise like a scream emerged from the center of the fighting. Cary cringed, frantically looking around. How the hell were they going to explain this when the cops finally showed up? Someone had to have called the police by now. Or animal control.

The flaming limb flailed about for a moment and then lay still, turning to ash in the intense heat of the magically made fire.

The fire sputtered a moment longer before winking out.

Kevin held very still. Not looking at Glen. His gaze firmly on the ashes.

Glen stared at the side of Kevin's face, his expression unreadable.

Cary wanted to jump in and explain or mitigate the damage or…do something to help, but she was afraid anything she said now would just make it worse.

Another scream, another shout, another hiss, and a series of blurred movements. Another tentacle arrowed right at Cary, like a missile slamming against her shield with a speed and ferocity that startled a teeth-clenched screech from her. The tentacle exploded against her shield in an impressive spray of blood and bits. She winced and looked away.

Glen and Kevin remained silently staring at each other.

When the monster itself quite suddenly slammed against Cary's shield, closer to the two men, its central mouth working madly as it strained toward them, they finally broke eye contact, jumping a little closer to Cary.

Without prompting, Kevin formed another fireball on the palm of his hand and threw it at the monster's head.

Cary's shield kept things from getting in. But it didn't prevent things from getting out.

The fireball engulfed the monster's entire head, the flames white hot this time.

The monster screamed, so loud she had to cover her ears. So loud, the shifters all stopped to cover their more sensitive ears. Intense, breath-stealing heat washed over her skin. And the stench of burning fat and oil was nothing she ever wanted to smell again.

The creature flailed against the fire, even as its head melted and an eye or two burst.

She had to close her eyes when that happened, which probably wasn't the best idea when there was a monster in front of her, but it was more grossness than she could handle. She set a hand to her stomach in a vain attempt to settle the rising nausea.

So much for her glorious dinner. If she saw another eye explode, she was going to toss up everything she'd eaten.

She opened her eyes but kept her gaze away from the monster as much as possible and scanned the surroundings, checking on the Joneses.

Dylan was holding his arm against his stomach. Caitlin helped one of her brothers—Owen, Cary thought—stand. Jocelyn, Michael, and Deacon stood just behind the monster, arrayed in a way that would prevent the creature from escaping down the street into the heart of the city.

She met Deacon's gaze. His eyes still glowed gold in the dark, his leopard near the surface but controlled.

Which was good. She wasn't sure if they had any spare clothes nearby for him if he shifted and ripped his clothes. And since he refused to use the magic that allowed him to reform those clothes— something she *just* learned he could do—he'd either have to walk through town in his big cat form, or he'd need to walk through town naked. Neither of which seemed a great way to remain inconspicuous.

Speaking of which, all the noise and stink had definitely drawn attention from the neighbors. Someone opened a door down the block. Another person watched through a window. Cary didn't see any cellphones but someone around here was getting a video of this, she was sure.

Shit.

The monster continued to flail. Refusing to die. Damn it. It kept tossing and throwing itself across the road. And Cary watched in horror when she realized some of the flames melting the monster's head were also dripping into areas with grass, landing in little burning lumps next to a sidewalk tree.

Her gaze jumped to all the surrounding houses. "Oh no."

Glen and Kevin looked at her, then looked at the monster, the flames leaping off its churning body.

"I don't suppose you do anything with ice or water," Cary said. The wizarding cat was out of the bag already, she might as well ask.

Kevin hesitated, which didn't bode well. Then Glen let out a long, slow breath and dipped his head. He began moving his hands in a small pattern and murmuring under his breath in a rhythm Cary realized was quite familiar. He sounded like her best friend Angie.

Like Angie reciting a spell.

A witch's spell.

The rain dropped suddenly and thick, so much pouring out of the sky all at once it blanketed the area and actually made it hard to see farther than a few feet away. The streetlights took on a misty quality and the houses blurred like paint running off a picture.

The stench of wet, burnt rubber overwhelmed her and she pressed a hand to her face to keep from gagging again.

The flames engulfing the monster slowly snuffed out, leaving a blackened and crackling mess in their wake.

The instant the fire died, Deacon leapt forward, Michael and Jocelyn at his back, and he tore the monster's crisped head off with his bare hands, flinging the huge body to one side of the road and the head to the other.

Glen met Kevin's gaze and with a little sigh, murmured something under his breath, another spell. A flash of lightning dropped from the clouds and slammed directly into what remained of the monster's head, sizzling across the already burnt mess and turning it to ash.

The rain slowed to a trickle before stopping completely.

For long moments, everyone remained silent, unmoving. And then, in the distance, the sounds of sirens.

Well shit.

6

____

ary met Deacon's gaze over the messy remains of wet ash and blackened…stuff from the monster. The thing was definitely dead now, none of its severed limbs continued to move. But there were still remnants of its body not turned to ash. And the stench of burnt rubber and lightning in the air continued to coat her tongue. All evidence of something no human first responder would be able to identify.

"What now?" she asked Deacon, slicking her wet hair back into her ponytail.

"We give them an excuse for all the noise," Maria said from Cary's side.

The sudden sound so close startled a squeak out of her. She put her hand to her heart and gave Maria a look. Maria released one of her slow, controlled smiles and shrugged slightly. She was soaked, like everyone else, but still managed to look elegant. Even her hair fell in lovely rivulets that were starting to bounce up into soft curls. How was it possible to get drenched and still look glamorous?

"You can think up an excuse for…" Cary gestured at the mess.

As she spoke, two of the Joneses, Owen and one of the middle sisters… What was her name? Brigit. That was it. Owen and Brigit picked up the remnants of the monster's body and flashed away into the woods.

"What are they doing?" Cary asked.

"Burying the evidence," Maria said, another quirk to her lips. She gestured to the ashes that had been the monster's head. They were rolling into the gutter with the run off from the deluge. "That will be gone soon. The body should remain down. But I'll contact one of the Families and make sure someone ensures that."

The sirens were getting closer.

"The monster not reanimating would be good," Cary said, glancing to the top of the street. "But people obviously saw what was happening. Probably took videos. How do we deal with that?"

"I'll get Nicky to scrub any evidence that appears on the web," Maria said.

"Nicky?" Nicky and Jillian were mates who'd been a great help to Cary last week, when she'd been stuck in the Jones mansion with nothing to wear to the charity ball. Unfortunately, the fancy dress Nicky had loaned her hadn't survived the kidnapping. But Deacon assured her he'd repaid Nicky. She'd never actually learned what either woman did for a living.

"She's a genius with all that…computer stuff," Maria said, a rare note of discomfort in her tone.

Deacon's very quiet chuckle made his mother's mouth flatten.

The sirens reached the top of the street and Cary could see the flashing red lights now as the police cars approached.

"You're a witch," Kevin said quietly to Glen.

The statement brought Cary's full attention back to her charges—who'd done the actual saving of the day.

"You're a wizard," Glen said.

"Have you known?"

Glen shook his head. "But I suspected."

"Why didn't you say anything? Why didn't you tell me you were a witch?"

"Our kind don't usual get along well," Glen said quietly, his gorgeous deep voice a murmured under the sounds of the sirens. "I was hoping I was wrong about… About the wizard thing."

"Now that you know?" Kevin asked, also very quietly.

Cary held her breath waiting for the answer, but she was foiled by the approaching police officers with guns drawn. Damn.

She moved to stand a little in front of everyone else. It meant she'd have to speak to the police, which she hated, but it also meant she could protect everyone from an "accidental" discharge of one of those guns if one of the cops got jumpy.

"What's going on here?" A man with a booming, commanding voice said from behind his raised gun.

Cary held her hands up. "What's wrong officer?"

She tried to look innocent, but she'd found when she did that people got more suspicious of her. She wasn't great at the whole lying thing. She was a lot better at irritating people. Which would be a bad strategy just then.

"We got a call about a violent incident. An animal on the loose." The officer straightened and lowered his weapon. But he didn't put it away.

A firetruck joined the cop cars at the top of the road.

Maria stepped up next to Cary. "Good evening, Officer Chen. How's your mother doing?"

The officer blinked and his gun went back into its holster. "Mrs. Jones. I didn't see you there."

He motioned to the other cops and they all put their weapons away as several of the firefighters left their truck and walked toward the gathering.

"What's going on here?" Officer Chen asked, his tone a lot less stern and accusatory now.

Cary tried not to marvel at the change too obviously.

"We were having a family dinner when we got an emergency call," Maria said with a shrug. "Someone thought they'd spotted a giant monitor lizard on the loose in the area."

"They called you instead of animal control?" Officer Chen sounded a little suspicious but not as suspicious as Cary would have assumed.

"Well, exotics are our specialty," Maria said with a shrug. "And the person who thought they'd seen the lizard had dealt with us before. You'll forgive them their leap over the heads of animal control I hope."

That last wasn't a question.

Officer Chen shuffled a little. "So long as no one was hurt, I'm sure it's fine. Was there a lizard?"

"Turned out there was. A Komodo lizard as a matter of fact."

Chen let out a loud whistle. "Those are huge, aren't they?"

"They can reach two hundred pounds and be very dangerous if not handled properly," Maria said.

Cary bit the inside of her cheek to keep quiet and just observe because this was some excellent "situation handling" and she should probably learn how to do this. She'd somehow managed to forget that she was with a family whose business was rescuing animals and since their specialty was exotic animals that maybe they could use that as an excuse here.

The monster might well have looked like an ordinary Komodo lizard to a bystander. If they didn't pay attention to the octopus head and tentacles.

But people would *believe* a Komodo dragon and convince themselves that's all they'd seen. Komodo dragons were real. Octopus-lizard monsters were not, according to most humans.

"Where's it now?" Chen searched the area, looking like he wanted to go for his gun again. Several of the other cops moved in tighter to Chen and also searched the area. The firefighters exchanged a frown.

"We were able to corral it and get it into one of our vans. It will be properly taken care of, and we'll find a good home for it. We'll need to look into how it got out, where it came from obviously. But we're used to handling this kind of thing."

Maria was spectacular. Cary was in awe. The woman didn't even blink. Didn't hesitate. Didn't stumble. She was a vision of capable control and calm. Even soaking wet.

"Good, good." Chen's shoulders relaxed again. "Glad to hear it." He frowned a little. "We also got reports of fire?"

"I'm not sure what that was about," Maria said. She gestured at the sky. "But after that downpour, if there had been a fire in this area, I'm sure it was snuffed out."

"We'd better look around," one of the firefighters called. "Just in case."

"Of course," Maria said. "I wouldn't want to think we'd missed something, with our attention focused on the lizard."

The firefighters spread out around the neighborhood, walking around and studying the street. Maria, Evan and Deacon moved closer to Chen to talk more about the "lizard." Owen and Brigit didn't return from the woods while the cops and firefighters were around, but if they'd been in trouble Cary was sure her Protector instincts would have gone off. She had to think they were staying in the woods to avoid more questions from the gathered humans.

All but one other cop returned to their cars and, with lights and sirens now off, left the area.

Cary moved closer to Glen and Kevin, since they were the reason she was here at all. "You two okay?" she murmured, keeping the firefighters and remaining two cops in her peripheral vision.

Kevin looked at Glen. "Are we?"

"Well, we're not dead," Glen said.

"And you saved the day with your skills," Cary felt the need to point out. "Both of you."

"You knew I was a wizard," Kevin said to her.

"I...had an idea. I'm not exactly unfamiliar with wizards. Or witches for that matter." She shrugged.

"Your friends." Kevin gestured to the Joneses. "They're not ordinary humans either."

"The world is full of interesting people, Kevin," she said, adopting her best philosophical tone. "So... You two. Not to be nosey, but I'm nosey, and I'm kind of hoping we didn't just save your lives only to end your relationship because you two looked really happy just before the monster attacked, and I know it's not my business, but..." She sighed. "I'm kind of a romantic, and I'd be sad if you broke up over the whole wizards and witches thing."

It was too much *Romeo and Juliet* tragedy for her.

"I think we have a lot to talk about," Glen said, his gaze on Kevin.

"Yeah, we do," Kevin said.

"But… Maybe." Both a statement and a question.

"Be nice to have someone to talk to about all this," Kevin said quietly. "Not having to keep the secret."

"Right?" Cary said. "It is. It's really nice." She pressed her lips together to avoid pushing any harder, a little surprised by her need to involve herself in trying to preserve their relationship.

Wisat had called Glen "the wizard's mate" and said he needed to survive, too. Maybe there was a reason for that. If Kevin was to go on and do great things, maybe he needed his witch mate to get there.

"We can talk more at home," Glen said.

And when he said "home" Kevin's shoulders relaxed visibly. "Yeah. Let's go home."

Cary waved goodbye to them as they turned back up the street, heading toward the main road. So they hadn't lived here. Just out for a walk. Wrong place at the wrong time. Poor guys. But maybe it had been worth it. If their relationship survived this upcoming conversation.

"They'll be fine," Deacon said from beside her.

She leaned into him as he wrapped his arms around her from behind, keeping her gaze on the two men as they walked off. "I hope so."

She turned in his arms to face him, taking in the rest of the situation as she did. The firefighters were returning to their truck. Officer Chen and the one other remaining cop were climbing into their car, Maria and Evan standing with them and saying goodbye.

"The situation looks handled," she said, still a little in awe of the ease. "Your family is good at that."

"We have had some practice," he said, kissing her forehead. "And fortunately, the Portland police haven't connected the events in Eugene last week with our family. They might eventually, but for now, every-thing is good."

She snuggled close, settling her head against his chest. His shirt was still damp, but his natural body heat had already dried it a little.

She was cold now that her adrenaline wasn't pumping and her Protector magic had stopped flowing. His warmth felt glorious. His arms tightened, and she sighed.

"Your family really knows how to throw a party," she said, chuckling under her breath.

"I'm not sure we've had a family dinner quite like this before."

"Yeah." She winced. "Sorry about that. I didn't expect them to follow."

"I should have, though." He shook his head, the movement brushing his cheek against the top of her head. "Next time you have to go out for a job during a family dinner, we'll try to keep them out of it."

"Probably be best." She looked up. "Anyone hurt?"

"Nothing that hasn't healed already."

That was good. She'd have felt really horrible if any of them had been seriously injured.

Caitlin joined them. "That was fun," she said with a grin. "You really know how to make a night interesting, Cary. I like that about you."

Cary snorted. "Sure. Thanks for everything. But maybe don't do it again. I'd hate for you guys to get hurt because of me."

"We're family. Of course we stick together." She grinned at Deacon and ambled off to join her brothers and sisters.

Leaving Cary gaping after her. Family?

They thought of her as part of their family? Already?

"Let's get home," Deacon said. "We need dry clothes. And I saved some leftovers for the dogs."

"My place then?"

"They're all staying at mine." Deacon nodded toward his gathered siblings and parents. "Do you want to stay there?"

"My house is good. We have to check on the dogs."

Was that panic in her voice? No. She was fine. This was all fine. Nothing to panic about.

Family?

Oh boy.

THANK YOU

Thank you for reading Dates, Dinners, and Other Disasters! I hope you enjoyed these short stories in the Cary Redmond world. For more short stories about our intrepid Protector, don't miss When Cary Met the Good Guys, an anthology of origin stories about when Cary met some of the most important people and pets in her life.

If this is your first introduction to Cary and her world, be sure to check out the main series, starting with The Trouble with Black Cats and Demons. And if you enjoy paranormal romance, my Tiger Shifters series is out now, starting with Once Upon a Tiger.

Don't forget to look out for the crossover paranormal romance novel between the Tiger Shifters and the Cary Redmond world, staring Deacon's youngest brother, Dylan. Romancing the Leopard releases in May 2021.

For more on my books, upcoming releases, and news, please subscribe to my newsletter (http://eepurl.com/OxQQL), visit my website (https://www.katsimons.com), or follow my author page at your favorite vendor.

Thanks again!

~Kat

BOOKS BY KAT SIMONS

THE CARY REDMOND SERIES

1 – The Trouble Black Cats and Demons

2 – The Trouble with Ghouls and Serial Killers

3 – The Trouble with Leopard Queens and Shifter Wars

4 – The Trouble with Baby Gods and Vampires

5 – The Trouble with Magic and Faery Curses

6 – The Trouble with Wizards and Old Enemies COMING SOON

CARY REDMOND SHORT STORIES

When Cary Met Jaxer

When Cary Met Pickles

When Cary Met Angie

When Cary Met Lucy

When Cary Met Marianne

Cary and Deacon (Try to) Go On A Date

Date Night Take Two

Third Date's the Charm

Cary vs the Goblin King

Dinner with the Jones

Cary and the Cursed Jack-o-Lantern

When Cary Met the Good Guys (Collection 1)

Dates, Dinners, and Other Disasters (Collection 2)

Romancing the Leopard: A Tiger Shifters-Cary Redmond Crossover Novel

TIGER SHIFTERS SERIES

1 – Once Upon a Tiger

2 – Along Came a Tiger

3 – Here There Be Tigers

4 – Her Tiger To Take

5 – To Tempt a Tiger

6 – Down Will Come Tiger

7 – To Catch a Tiger

8 – What a Tiger Wants

9 – Taming Her Tiger

Tiger Shifters Series Vol 1 (Books 1 - 3)

Tiger Shifters Series Vol 2 (Books 4 - 6)

JOAN OF KERRY SERIES

1 – Joan of Kerry: Joan and the Abhartach

ABOUT THE AUTHOR

Kat Simons earned her Ph.D. in animal behavior, working with animals as diverse as dolphins and deer. She brought her experience and knowledge of biology to her paranormal romance and urban fantasy fiction, where she delights in taking nature and turning it on its ear. Her Tiger Shifters series combines romance and the otherworldly with heart-pounding action adventure. Her latest urban fantasy romance series follows the adventures of Protector Cary Redmond as she tries to manage her personal life while saving the world. A lot.

For something a little different, Kat also publishes fantasy romance, science fiction romance, and the occasional hockey romance under the name Isabo Kelly (http://www.isabokelly.com).

After traveling the world, Kat now lives in New York City with her family. She is a stay-at-home mom and a full time writer.

For more on Kat and her future books:

Website: https://www.katsimons.com
Newsletter: http://eepurl.com/OxQQL

www.ingramcontent.com/pod-product-compliance
Lightning Source LLC
Chambersburg PA
CBHW030754200726
48288CB00004B/1165